To Merrily

May you always celebrate life!

Best wishes,
Joanne C. Beinst

Loss
and How to Cope with It

Houghton Mifflin/Clarion Books/New York

Joanne E. Bernstein

LOSS
and How to Cope with It

ACKNOWLEDGMENTS
The passage from *Cavett* by Dick Cavett and Christopher Porterfield was reprinted by permission of Harcourt Brace Jovanovich, Inc.

The passages from "The *Writer's Digest* Interview: Ray Bradbury" by Robert Jacobs originally appeared in the February 1976 issue of *Writer's Digest* and are reprinted by permission of the publisher.

Houghton Mifflin/Clarion Books
52 Vanderbilt Avenue, New York, NY 10017

Copyright © 1977 by Joanne E. Bernstein. All rights reserved. No part of this book may be reproduced or transmitted in any form or by any means, electronic or mechanical, including photocopying, recording, or any information storage and retrieval system, without permission in writing from the publisher.
Printed in the United States of America

Library of Congress Cataloging in Publication Data

Bernstein, Joanne E.
  Loss and how to cope with it.
    "A Clarion book."
    Includes index.
    SUMMARY: An exploration of how the death of a loved one affects the survivors with practical discussion of how to handle the many emotional and physical reactions we may encounter in bereavement.
    1. Bereavement—Psychological aspects—Juvenile literature. [1. Death—Psychological aspects. 2. Grief] I. Title.
BF575.G7B48   155.9'37'024054   76-50027
ISBN 0-395-28891-6   Paperback ISBN 0-395-30012-6

(Previously published by The Seabury Press under ISBN 0-8164-3189-2)

Second Printing

Cover illustration by Neil Waldman

For Michael

Contents

Introduction	1
1. What Happens When Someone Dies	3
2. Your Ideas about Death	18
3. Your Feelings	31
4. You Can Handle Your Feelings	45
5. When Someone Special Dies	65
6. The Many Ways of Death	82
7. Living with the Survivors	96
8. The Legacy of Survivors	109
9. Some Final Words	117
Further Reading	121
Advanced Study	130
Films about Death	135
Service Organizations and Sources for Information	138
Life Events Scale	144
Index	146

Introduction

To live is to know loss.

Human existence begins and ends with change and separation, the major determinants of loss. At life's start, each of us is thrust from our mother's womb into an unknown world. At life's end, we encounter the biggest separation of all, as we must depart, in death, from everything we cherish.

In between birth and death, we are destined for an almost continuous series of changes, large and small. Since part of us always resists changes, even when we have chosen them, we react with strong emotion. That response is called loss. The range of response is broad, including sorrow, joy, anger, and a host of other possibilities. After we react to change, we then assess the situation and make adjustments.

What is loss?

Loss is our resentment when a younger sibling follows us onto the scene. We are no longer the center of attention.

Loss is the loneliness suffered as we leave the security of the family circle for school. We wonder if there will be friendly faces to greet us.

Loss is the disruption we fear if our parent changes jobs and we must start all over again in another town.

Loss is the hollowness we feel if we are left out when others are invited to parties.

Loss is our confusion during moments we can't find something—a watch, homework, a favorite shirt.

Loss is the sadness and self-doubt we endure when we are forced to give up goals. Physics attracts us as a career, but algebra gives us trouble; we dream of playing in a symphonic orchestra, but our talents on the flute aren't good enough to make the school band.

Even if we've been totally unique and have rarely been disappointed, we know loss simply because throughout life we're always growing. And growth means change.

If to live is to know loss, then it makes sense to learn as much about it as possible. This book concerns one of life's greatest losses, the death of a loved one. However, the information applies to other types of loss as well.

Each of us can prepare for the separations and changes that we will encounter. Loss cannot be ignored, for it will not go away. Each loss must be faced, grappled with, and managed. Then we can survive, celebrate existence, and deal effectively with each new experience. With so much of living entwined with losing, the way we cope with loss is one indicator of the way we cope with life.

1

What Happens When Someone Dies

The 1970s are a wonderful time for learning about death and loss. Previously, these subjects were viewed as unpleasant, and they were avoided. There were so many unanswered questions: What is it like to die? When are we really dead? What happens after death? Why must we die? As the only animals with the intelligence to realize we would eventually succumb, the image of our own extinction frightened us.

Today, thanks to a growing number of explorers, we are beginning to learn some of the answers to these very difficult questions. Investigators have joined together from such diverse fields as psychology, medicine, education, the ministry, and mortuary science. Their work has brought death and loss out of hiding and into the arena of everyday conversation.

Before the last several years, dying and loss were rarely mentioned in all of formal schooling. Now, many schools and colleges offer courses in the area. Also, an increasing number of books dealing with death are finding their way to bookshelves and bestseller lists.

Learning about death will make us more comfortable with its eventuality. Marcus Aurelius said, "It is not death that man should fear, but he should fear never beginning to live."

What Is Death?

The human body consists of exquisitely designed systems which function with marvelous synchronization. In most cases, these intricate networks have the strength and capability to overcome attack, keeping the organism whole and living. With the help of medical science, that capability to survive is made even greater, and people are living longer and longer. Modern machinery can keep life going even if the body or mind has been ravaged by disease or other forms of breakdown.

With the advances in medical science, the question of what constitutes death is no longer a simple matter. Scientific and philosophic controversies arise: When is a person really dead? At what point is there no hope for recovery and return to a normal life?

Today, the dilemma of medical death is still not resolved, but many doctors lean toward declaring a person dead when the brain has ceased producing brain waves and there is no hope for reversing the damage. The brain can stop functioning for several reasons, because it is supported by many other organs and systems in the body. If one of these stops working and cannot be medically repaired or substituted for, the brain will die. For example, the brain needs oxygen. Oxygen is carried by the blood, and the blood cannot get around to the various parts of the body without the heart to pump it. If the heart breaks down, oxygen-rich blood cannot reach the brain, and it will eventually die.

Upon brain death, the brain impulses that regulate the function of all body systems cease and, in turn, each system shuts down: death is the result. Our experiences tell us that a dead person is never again seen on earth, at least not in recognizable form. The body does not go on a journey or enter permanent sleep. The body does not react to stimulus.

And After Death–A Funeral

If you accept this description of death, then you can see that after a person dies, the death is really only the concern of those who survive. And, like births and weddings, a family death is one of the most important events in its history. It must be marked, for its effects will keenly alter family life and can have an impact beyond the bounds of the family.

Before a person dies, preferences might be expressed for specific plans to follow death, such as burial in the country, or elimination of flowers at the funeral. After death, these requests may be honored. However, the responses of those remaining also determine the nature of what happens next.

Most people express a desire for a funeral or memorial meeting. This usually coincides with the wishes of survivors, and in most places around the world such a ceremony is planned. A funeral usually takes place within a week after death, and the body is present. A memorial meeting is conducted without the body and can take place at any time after death. It may include a religious service, or it may not.

After a death, even if death were expected, the close survivors feel great shock. If you have been a survivor, you know a feeling of being transported to another world in which daily events don't exist and death predominates. In this new world, you feel out of place and incomplete, part of your equipment for dealing with each day has been taken from you. With the death, you have lost a great portion of yourself.

The shock you go through is felt as sharply by adult survivors. Scheduling and attending a funeral or memorial meeting helps survivors of all ages to come to grips with their distress.

This is true in places all over the world. However, the variation in customs from group to group influences the way they cope with their feelings of loss. For example, the Kota Indian tribe will conduct two funerals for each person who dies—one for the family and another for the community. The amount of emotion expressed at these two events enables the tribe to view death without denying its existence.

In the United States and elsewhere, a vocation has evolved specifically to help survivors through the physical and emotional upheaval which immediately trails death. Called morticians, funeral directors, or undertakers, they perform many needed community services.

Morticians transport the body from place of death to a mortuary. There they prepare it for burial or other disposal. The body may be embalmed, or temporarily preserved, which involves replacing blood and other fluids with special embalming fluid that forestalls decomposition. After consulting the family, morticians make arrangements for the funeral ceremony and burial. Morticians also help families by caring for necessary legal matters, such as obtaining death certificates from the state.

The funeral industry has been criticized widely, with morticians characterized as overly anxious to take advantage of the emotional state of bereavement. High-pressure tactics and exorbitant prices are jokingly called the "high cost of leaving."

Without doubt, some representatives of the funeral business do cheat consumers. Fearing that if they pay attention to death, it will beckon them, most customers purchasing funeral packages have done little or no previous comparison shopping. They are easy marks for those who wish to intimidate. But when morticians do their jobs well (and many, many do), it is because they realize that whatever the location, whatever the style, the ceremony is an opportunity to acknowledge the passing of life: It is an occasion of powerful significance.

The procedures of a funeral vary from place to place. The ceremony may be preceded by a day or more of visiting in the funeral home. At this time, people come to express their sorrow. The funeral itself may take place in either the funeral home, the person's place of worship, or even the person's actual home.

Services are likely to include prayer, one or more talks

about the life of the person who has died, and possibly some music. The memorial meeting will be similar, but it will lack the visual focus upon the casket, which is an important part of the funeral procedure, reinforcing death's unquestionable truth.

At a funeral or memorial, the participants have a chance to express bereavement and say good-bye. If you are among them, it's a time to celebrate the contributions and unique qualities of the person you knew. A ceremony allows you to come to terms with the trauma of death, to be persuaded of its reality.

The funeral is an opportunity to get together with others who are affected by the death, drawing support from the bonds you share. The setting reminds you that you are part of a larger world. Within it there exists continuity of life. It is a memorial, and you remember.

At a funeral, you may cry. While there may be tears, there can also be moments of happiness. You may be comforted to see how many people have come to be with you and show they care about you.

You may also feel anger. Enraged at a world that seems mercilessly unjust, you may answer death with fury. This is especially true if the person who has died was not very old or if death could have been avoided.

The drama of a funeral unfolds from the force of many different emotions. One of these is fear. Some people fear everything that concerns death, dreading funerals especially.

Joshua was already in college when death first touched him closely. His Uncle Stan, a printer, was dead. Suddenly Joshua was called upon to attend his first funeral service. For two days before the event, he threw up the little he could eat. On the train home, Joshua recognized where his feelings came from: Someday he, too, would die. His mind was dizzy with thought. He wanted to run. How he hated to see people cry! He just knew there'd be crying at the service. It might even make him cry. And what if his uncle's body were shown? Would he look at him? Should he?

The funeral itself wasn't nearly as bad as Joshua had imagined it. As the ceremony progressed, Joshua was relieved and impressed that he could get through it. He also observed that he wasn't the only terrified person in the room. Many of his cousins looked scared, and so did his own parents. He wasn't alone.

One of the speakers at the funeral, another uncle, guided the audience toward meeting their own eventual mortality. In concluding, he reminded them of what the Bible says (Eccles. 3:1),

> To everything there is a season
> and a time to every purpose . . .
> A time to be born, a time to die;
> A time to cry, and a time to laugh.

Joshua gave thought to the cycle of life. His uncle was dead, but Joshua still lived. "Yes, our relationship is over," he said to himself, and looked at his uncle's body to confirm it and convince himself.

Joshua thought about the importance of each being on earth and the significance of each day in molding a life. "There was pain in my uncle's life, but there were also many wonderful years. I have many years to go. I suppose mine will be a mixture, too."

Joshua was struck by the imposing strength and impact of his thoughts. He decided that perhaps the majesty of life was the reason his first funeral was accompanied by a degree of pomp and circumstance. It resembled a solemn parade, complete with stately music and rituals performed in orderly fashion. Joshua was carried away by its beauty.

Many adults aren't sure if you, as a young person, should attend funerals and memorial meetings. Psychiatrists, such as Dr. John Schowalter of Yale University, feel that children of any age who request to attend the memorial for a close person should be permitted to do so. Young people over nine should be encouraged to go.

Attending brings you into the center of things, to share and express the sadness of a critical family event. Not being allowed to go can lead you to imagine rites that are more frightening than reality. Think of Joshua.

Before going, ask someone to explain what happens at a funeral. Find out the reasons behind each custom. Even Joshua, at age eighteen, wasn't sure of what to expect and was scared. It's helpful for you to know what you'll see, what you should do, and who'll be along for company.

What Next?

After the funeral, it is time to dispose of the body. If burial is chosen, the casket is taken to a cemetery where it is deposited either in a grave in the ground or in a mausoleum aboveground. A tombstone marks the place. If you've never walked through a cemetery, you might consider it. You may find a cemetery pleasantly verdant, not ghostridden. Looking over the gravestones of generations, even centuries of your forebears, you may find food for thought.

Burial offers an opportunity for rituals that can help speed our acceptance of loss. In Samoa, for example, the dead are anointed before burial. This practice, in which the body is examined, reinforces the permanence of death. Embalming, on the other hand, preserves the image of life as it was, perhaps masking the reality of death and leaving us without the harsh confrontation of its finality.

Within the casket, the body slowly decomposes, as the cells are broken down by bacteria. The body is totally unaware of surroundings and feels nothing.

Most people in the United States choose burial as the method for disposal. Another way to do it is cremation. When a body is cremated, it is taken to a crematorium and there, heat reduces the body to ashes and small pieces of bone. It doesn't hurt. Again, nothing is felt by the dead person.

After cremation, survivors receive the remains in an urn or box. These might be scattered over a body of water or over the ground. Remains can be saved, either in a home or in a part of the crematorium devoted to the preservation of remains, called the columbarium. They can also be buried in an urn garden.

Cremation is a very ancient practice, based on the belief that burning is the only way a soul can escape the body to continue functioning. Today, cremation is not always chosen for religious reasons. Some people feel it is simpler. Some are concerned about diminishing land supply on earth. Others don't believe in visiting cemeteries. And still others feel the remains of the dead should nurture a place that gave pleasure in life. That's the way it was when Marge's grandmother died. She'd been a robust hiker and had walked the ridges of most of the ranges in the western United States. A fine hiker herself, Marge had accompanied her to the Rockies. Upon the woman's death, a trip was planned so that her remains could be returned to the Teton Range, one of her grandmother's favorite places on earth.

Whether the person you cared for is buried or cremated, it's comforting to realize that all elements in the world never disappear. Instead, the remains of the dead continue to contribute to the life cycle. In Helen Coutant's book, *First Snow,* a Vietnamese girl watches with wonder as snowflakes rapidly change to drops of water. It's impossible to catch them, but it is drops such as those that have helped a pine sapling to reach thumbsize. "The drop of water had not really gone; it had only changed, like the snowflake, into something else. 'You will change, too,' Liên spoke to the tiny tree, 'but not yet.' "

Questions of the Soul
We know that the snowflake changes but doesn't disappear. We know that the body, when dead, changes but

doesn't disappear. It is the hope of many human beings that their inner beings also will not disappear upon their deaths but will continue to exist.

We can't truly imagine our own extinction. Certainly no one has yet been able to tell us what it's like. You may wonder if it's painful to die, for instance.

Fifteen-year-old Iris doesn't think so. Her mother suffered from cancer for several years. There was pain in her illness. Iris was particularly disturbed by her mother's breathlessness and sleepless nights. Yet, when her mother died, Iris and all the others at the bedside noticed that strain from the long ordeal had drained from the woman's face. She looked peaceful in death, even happy.

Over the years, that harmony has been reported repeatedly by those who look upon death. Stirred by this observation, researchers such as Dr. Elisabeth Kübler-Ross and Dr. Raymond Moody have studied hundreds of people who have been either nearly dead or actually clinically dead but have lived to tell about their experience. Consistently, their subjects speak of peace and wholeness—and painlessness. They come out of these episodes unafraid to die.

This new research may one day offer partial information concerning what happens to the soul after death. The soul, or spirit, is the term for the personal qualities and characteristics of each living person.

Over the centuries, we have tried to fill in the pieces of information about an afterlife that are missing. In all aspects of art, in religion, in the recesses of the human mind, and now in science, we search and hope for whatever follows death. In ancient Greece, Plato called that something more a reality higher than the physical realm.

In the present studies, the people who have experienced "death" have reported phenomena that would hint at a modified but continuing existence after death. They speak of floating out of the body, retaining awareness of things going on around them, but being unable to communicate. Some see their life histories flash before them, and many see a warm, loving light beckoning them.

At this point, it cannot be said with certainty that this beginning research reveals accurate information about death. Perhaps it merely informs about alterations in the brain and hallucinations of people who are overwhelmed by illness or life-threatening accident. Nevertheless, for many, reality beyond death is part of an outlook on life. Some claim that reality is called heaven. In fact, adults who don't believe in heaven themselves often tell their children about it. This might reveal their desire to shield youngsters from loss. Or it might indicate the true depth and scope of humanity's search for immortality.

Heaven and immortality are viewed in many ways. Some of our impressions come from literature. In Virginia Lee's *The Magic Moth,* a young girl named Maryanne dies of heart disease. At the moment of her death, a beautiful moth escapes from its cocoon, creating a symbolic demonstration of the continuity of life, which hints at afterlife.

Some psychologists look at heaven as less of a reality

and more of an expression of a need for security felt by those on earth. With a place assigned for spirits of the dead, survivors can keep the dead somewhat alive, yet out of reach.

A Religious View

Life after death is contemplated by theologians of all persuasions. Christians conceive of the road to eternal life as a central focus within the religion, seeing devotion to Jesus as requisite. Within Christianity, however, there are differences among sects.

Protestants feel that God lovingly accompanies a person both in life and in death. If one has loved God, hope for eternal life in heaven becomes more assured.

Catholics also emphasize God's love. Death is perceived as the will of God. Catholics regard attainment of eternal life as a goal that shapes patterns of behavior and religious standards. If merited, eternal life is characterized by an ecstatic fulfilled state of oneness with God in heaven.

Some religious Jews believe in life after death for the soul, without viewing it as reward. Other Jews are unsure about events after death and rely upon the justice of God's ways. They emphasize living well and leave themselves in His hands.

Followers of many Eastern religions believe in immortality. As their concepts do not stem from Judeo-Christian heritage, their picture of life after death is different from that of Christians and Jews. Many Hindus, for example, stress the circle of life, a cycle that includes rebirth on earth. It is believed that the soul lives anew in another creature. The type of creature the soul comes back in is based upon the quality of the previous life. As a consequence, in some Eastern religions, animals are holy.

The beliefs of both Western and Eastern religious groups have impact upon all of us. In each is found profound regard for the unique dignity and worthiness of every human being. That perspective reaches believers and non-believers alike, making the death of any person an event of significance.

The Condolence Call

It is customary in many parts of the world to pay a condolence call after someone has died. Relatives, friends, neighbors, and acquaintances come to the home of the bereaved family. Some come immediately upon hearing of the death, while others wait until after burial or cremation has taken place.

Most customs come about because they have social value. This one is no different. If you are bereaved, having people visit helps you to feel connected to the living. It tells you that others comprehend what you are going through, want to be with you, and will help if they can. For you it is a chance to go over the details of your loved one's death with different visitors, relieving yourself of some of your hurt.

Not everyone who enters your home for a condolence call is well known to you. It may seem odd that people your relative hardly knew have suddenly taken an interest. This happens because each of us is affected by every death we hear of. John Donne said, "No man is an island. . . . Any man's death diminishes me, because I am involved in Mankinde."

Whether you are Catholic, Protestant, or Jew; Moslem, Buddhist, or Hindu; believer or non-believer—within your lifetime some of your loved ones will die. It is inevitable that one day you will die, too. Death is indeed a mystery. But some things are certain. As expressed in Ecclesiastes (1:4), "One generation passeth away, and another generation cometh: and the earth abideth forever."

2

Your Ideas about Death

Death is the end of life, the final chapter. It is the natural fate for all living things.

Everyone knows that, you say. If you think about it, though, you realize it is not so. You were not born knowing all life must end, and your journey toward understanding has been a long one.

If you weren't born knowing about death, but you are aware of it now, just how did you find out?

Concepts Grow and Change

Your introductions to death have come slowly. As the years progress, you learn to adjust to the deaths in your life (including your own) because you have many chances to manage smaller separations. Some of these are temporary, such as going to camp. Others are permanent, such as losing your baby teeth, or leaving high school upon graduation. These separations are dwarfed next to the prospect of losing someone in death. The smaller separations prepare you as best they can by providing understanding.

Psychologists believe that you become aware of temporary separations first, starting when you are still an infant. In a sense, the daily rhythm of being asleep and then awake is a first lesson in death. Babies, of course, have not developed a sound idea of the passage of time. As a result, they cannot imagine the eternity of death. They know only absence, as when the family is downstairs and they lie alone in their cribs upstairs. All babies notice that their parents go away and return, but they do not know enough about time to recognize a clear pattern. They immaturely try to think through what is going on, but are hindered by their lack of words as tools of thought.

In attempts to test their beginning ideas, infants make up their own separation games. No doubt you have seen infants and toddlers play peek-a-boo. You have also seen them gleefully throw toys out of their high chairs and playpens. In both games, their greatest pleasure is in the reappearance of the person or object that has been absent. You probably have noticed that they almost never tire of this game. To their parents' dismay, they can go on with the game repeatedly—twenty, thirty, forty times. Moderate patience shown by parents and siblings during this time is a good thing. Through the games, the babies are learning that some separations, though necessary, are temporary. They combine their conclusions from the games with what they have experienced after their sleep periods and reassure themselves that they will be cared for. They can rest comfortably.

Soon after babies become aware that some things disappear and then return, they begin to notice that some things go away and never do reappear. This, too, becomes cause for investigation, and the games which follow can be much more frustrating for parents than peek-a-boo and drop-the-toy.

In order to explore objects that never return, babies take to the most obvious sources. This is the time when parents constantly find their children's hands at trash cans and the toilet flush system (if not in the bowl itself). In each case they are depositing something which they gradually learn they will not get back. Babies and parents everywhere seem to call this "all gone." In the spirit of experimentation, babies sometimes devise other games that demonstrate permanent absence. You may have seen toddlers drink their glasses dry, turn them upside down, and joyfully shout the refrain, "All gone."

Parents are wise to allow their babies to satisfy their curiosity about trash cans, toilets, and the like. Allowed to inquire with supervision, toddlers begin their lifetime mastery of that other kind of separation—permanent separation. The second lesson about death has begun. The child is on the journey toward knowledge of death: that it exists, that it is the final stage of life, and that it befalls everyone.

Unfortunately, the journey is a slow one. In a well-known study, Dr. Maria Nagy interviewed hundreds of Hungarian children about their views of death. She found out that children cannot truly see death as permanent until they are about five years old. Youngsters of three, four, and even five tend to view death as changed life. They see life in death and are unable to separate life from death.

Children of this age may view the dead as less alive or possibly asleep. They may think the dead exist in a different form within the grave or in another place. They may imagine that dead people need food or that they continue to be in on the comings and goings of those who live. Finally, they sometimes think that the dead may return.

An example of children's responses at this age was seen in a young boy named Andrew. At three, he knew two men named Lou. The fact that his grandfather and a family friend had the same name amazed and amused him no end. Andrew's confusion about death became evident a week after his grandfather died. Andrew's mother was speaking with friend Lou on the telephone. "Hello, Lou," she said. Andrew rushed eagerly to the phone. "Is that Grandpa Lou calling from heaven?" he asked.

There is good reason for young children to feel that death is altered life. Think back to your own life at three and four or look at preschool children you now know. You will see that boys and girls of this age group view the entire world as existing for them alone, almost like a gigantic present inviting exploration. In keeping with that image, they also decide somewhere along the line that they are responsible for some of the earth's wonders. As a result of this magical idea of self, you might hear a young boy say that the sun goes away when he pulls down the window shade. Or you might hear a toddler squeal for flying birds to return, clearly thinking that her calls have power.

Children, who see life almost exclusively in terms of

themselves, do not find it easy to imagine anything totally unlike themselves. They have learned enough about life to know that they themselves are alive. Many things must be like them, they reason. Even mountains are alive, they say. They cannot begin to extend their thoughts to something so opposite to life as death. They will concede that the dead are less alive, but totally gone? Inconceivable.

Years of living bring with them further experiences, and the journey gradually includes comprehension that death is a permanent state. By the time they are five or six, children have become less occupied with themselves and their central position in the world. Their universe is now larger than the family alone. Also, by this time, they have endured additional separations. Some have been temporary, such as going to school for the first time. Others have been permanent, such as watching insects or pets die. In addition, children have heard of deaths of neighbors and older relatives, and some may even have mourned for a death in the family.

Children of about five or six review their experiences and observe several things. They note that things happen apart from them and without their involvement. In other words, the sun will rise or set even if they never approach the window shade. Children also note that the dead do not return. They then slowly put two and two together and change their minds, concluding that death is in no way reversible.

Such a judgment is hard to take for adults as well as

children. But, from when they discover the truth at about five up until about the age of nine, children have a fascinating way of adjusting to it. Nagy's research showed that youngsters cope by keeping death outside the door, weaving a web of protection for themselves. Some children in the early grades of school will speak of a death-man or death-angel, a being who is seen for a brief moment as it carries a person off. They imagine that while death is a reality, they can trick it or run to escape its grasp.

Hiding is what two eight-year-old girls had in mind when they spent the night of President John Kennedy's death under a bed. Their parents didn't understand their actions, and neither did they. The two couldn't explain, but they felt safe only there.

Safety from the death-carrier was also in the mind of a sick girl who expressed her thoughts in pictures. Janie was suffering from leukemia, a condition in which white blood cells go haywire within the blood and multiply wildly. It is a type of cancer about which doctors and scientists have been able to learn a great deal. Increasingly, leukemia is curable or at least arrestable. Janie was hoping for cure in her drawing of a group of little children running from a massive white blood cell that threatened to engulf them. She said that the cell was called "Death."

Some children in the younger grades do not imagine a death-carrier or seek protection from it. But they do try to keep death outside themselves. In a recent study, Dr. Gerald Koocher, an American psychologist, asked children of this age group what would happen to them at the time of their deaths. While not speaking of a death-angel, they hinted that they, too, try to keep death at a distance. One way such youngsters have been reassured is by learning about death. They ask many questions, trying to get as much information as they can about dying, funerals, and cemeteries. They are only sorry that they cannot unravel the mystery totally through communication with the dead. The best they can do is amass technical knowledge, and this seems to provide confidence to face the future.

The accumulation of honest information would seem to speed the journey along. Sometime around age nine, Nagy found that children usually forsake the death-man and the idea that death is outside of themselves. They begin to conclude that death is not only permanent, it is also universal. Children of this age realize that death is not governed by a death-person but is a natural part of life, governed by laws of the universe.

They now know that they, too, will die. At this point, it can be said that children's understanding of death is quite like that of an adult. The years have given most nine-year-olds a wide range of confrontations with temporary and permanent separation. What they have learned from these provides the base for comprehending the nature of further separations, including death. If they have been lucky and have lived in families where bereavement is accepted and mourning encouraged, young people will probably go on to meet their future separations with continued love for life.

The Child Remains Within the Adult

Not everyone is lucky. The journey toward accepting death and allowing mourning is a lifetime struggle for many. We may say out loud that death means the end of physical life, but the whys and wherefores of death remain such a mystery that we don't always act as though we are convinced. Even adults return to children's ways of looking at death now and then. If adults cling to childlike concepts, it becomes harder for the children close to them to develop mature concepts about death.

Adults show reluctance to give up the notions of childhood in several ways. Some are helpful, some are not. After a death in the family, many will say, "rest in peace." In this case, if they envision a body resting, older people may be expressing the idea that the dead are less alive. They are comforting themselves, and this may have value. On the other hand, holding onto childlike responses may also bring with it severe discomfort. Have you ever heard someone fret over a dead loved one who must "suffer" in the cold earth through rain and snow? Such people may remind themselves that the dead person feels nothing, but they cannot rid their minds of worry.

Adults can express childlike ideas about death in other ways. Some grownups conduct their lives in ways which announce that, like children, they, too, must keep death outside themselves. They will not talk about death, as though not talking will make it go away, and they put off decisions and plans that might cause them to admit their own mortality. At times, this behavior endangers the security of a group of people. You may have known of families like the Harringtons, who were astounded when Mr. Harrington, the only one working at the time, died and left them without life insurance or a proper will. It was many months before his survivors could put financial matters in order. After all their running back and forth in banks and courts, they realized they'd lost a lot of funds and energy that were needed elsewhere. For years, they had all refused to look at the possibility of his death.

Denying the inevitability of death is one of the reasons such things are allowed to happen.

Death as a Hidden Embarrassment

Without doubt, it is hard to be mature about death. It is made even harder because death is often hidden, and this, too, works against a mature concept of death.

Medical knowledge keeps most of us living longer. That is wonderful, of course, but fewer deaths exist for us to learn from. When deaths do occur, we are often unable to be a part of them. City dwellers cannot see the normal life and death cycle of a farm. Today's children can be separated from their grandparents by hundreds or thousands of miles, seeing them infrequently. When these older relatives die, the deaths may appear as remote incidents that do not bring with them bereavement. In addition, these days when a death takes place in the immediate family, the person rarely dies at home. There is likely to be hospitalization, in part to receive medical care, in part to prevent a disturbing scene within the home setting. For adults, the hospital death eases the impact of loss. For children, the hospital death may ease the impact almost to the point of erasure, since children are deliberately and specifically excluded from hospitals.

We hide our ill and we hide our aged people, too. Both are closer to death. Perhaps we do this because we regard death as an embarrassment, an insult, an accident, surely an unnatural event. This is in direct contrast to a mature idea of death, but it becomes understandable if we look at today's life.

Here we are, in a society where we can send people to the moon with hardly an error. We can view events around the world as they are happening. We can even store whole libraries of information in a computer the size of an automobile. In a society that can produce such wonders, it *is* upsetting to reflect that we haven't been able to conquer disease, old age, and the final mystery of death. In response, we segregate those who remind us. We do not speak of our embarrassment over cancer, heart disease, and death. We turn questions away. We hesitate to mourn in public. We even make up words to cover what has happened. "He passed away," we say. Death is the final taboo.

Attempts to hide the truth try to give the impression that we live in an almost deathless world—if not deathless, at least death is far away. The attempts fall short, though, and merely leave a bewildering illusion.

Television and movies do little to relieve confusion. Instead, they intensify it and give it new turns. By the age of twelve, anyone who has access to these media has seen countless news and entertainment shows in which killings, crashes, and wars form a central core. One would have to be deaf and blind not to absorb knowledge of these events. Yet it is not long before children realize that deaths in the entertainment shows are staged by actors. The killings on the news are so numerous that they, too, take on an unreal quality. It would be overwhelming no matter what age to watch the news if each individual death had to be seriously contemplated. We defend ourselves with an imaginary shield so that we can continue to watch what is real. The confusion is made even worse for children by the presence of violent television cartoons. In cartoons, people and animals are put through ordeals that would appear to maim or kill. In spite of falling from a cliff or being electrocuted, the characters get right up to do battle once more. It is easy to see why death is often viewed as unreal.

Misinformation Can Hurt

Some people add still further to confusion. Their embarrassment about death is so great that they cannot deal honestly with questions. Parents who tell children that their dead loved one is asleep are trying to protect them. They do no one a favor. Seven-year-old George was told his uncle had gone to sleep. For many nights, George refused to go to sleep, afraid of what lurked in the darkness. Finally his mother caught on and gently tried to undo the damage. Many evening hours were spent at George's bedside, reading stories and sharing the day's happenings. Two months went by before George was back to his natural habits.

Some parents try to bring comfort by relating that the dead person has gone away on a trip. Children then may sadly conclude that they were abandoned for a better family or a happier existence. They might yearn to take the pilgrimage, too. That is what happened to Alma. When she was nine, her father died. Her mother was at a loss to explain his sudden, unexpected death and compared it to a wandering adventure. Alma thought more and more about the joy of her father's adventure. She had a series of accidents, each more serious than the last. A psychologist pointed out that Alma's feelings of sadness had become desperate and her accidents were actually attempts to join her father in death. If parents knew that children could feel and act this way, they would not speak of death as a trip.

Religious beliefs can bring comfort in the face of death. Religious people often see a higher purpose to life, which helps them make sense of what goes on around them. God is the force in their lives that makes the whole thing come together, the presence that makes it easier to cope with problems large and small.

While religious beliefs can console, sometimes adults phrase their convictions in ways that may not be helpful to children. Stacey's family used such phrases. When her beloved Aunt Sylvia died, her mother tried to comfort her by saying, "God wanted Aunt Sylvia to come live with him in Heaven." Her father said it slightly differently, "God took Aunt Sylvia." Both hoped to ease Stacey's sense of loss and make her more religious, but they wound up doing just the opposite. Stacey, a thoughtful girl of ten, asked herself about God. "What kind of God is this?" she said. "Who is this God, who can strike anyone down without fair warning?" As happens all too often, she answered the questions with fear and anger toward God.

In recent years, officials of some churches have informed their worshippers about the dangers of making God appear as a cruel taskmaster. Some have suggested calming ways to express the importance of God in the cycle of life and death. For instance, the Methodists recommend saying that we are surrounded by God's love in life and death.

Your journey toward understanding and accepting death is indeed a long and hard one. Knowing how your ideas about death were formed can be useful in seeing where the obstacles to understanding exist in your life in order to diminish or eliminate them. Until we openly admit that death is the natural and final episode in life, the journey toward understanding is not complete. Only when we fully accept the eventual end can we begin to celebrate life properly.

3

Your Feelings

Your life has been turned upside down. A person or pet you loved was alive one day and dead the next. You and your world will never be the same. Even years from now, you will remember it as one of the most important and unfortunate events ever to occur in your life.

You are not alone by any means. Many young people lose someone dear because of death. Yet death embarrasses many adults and sometimes they cannot discuss it fully. You may be left puzzled and curious about the sudden and overwhelming things that are happening to you.

The time after a loved one dies is called bereavement, because of the many changes in the way you feel. Bereavement is the name for a state of being—the way you are after a valued object or person has been taken from you.

The bereavement time begins with the terrible shock of losing the person or object. It continues until the loss of the person or object is understood and accepted. The bereavement period when a family member dies lasts a long time, often a year or more. The signs of bereavement can be seen both in your body and your mind. You feel and act very differently from the way you do normally. In fact, you may feel so unlike yourself that you wonder if you will ever return to your usual habits. You ask yourself if your pain, called grief, will ever go away.

The pain of bereavement is a state of slow healing, as you head toward accepting the fact that you have lost something valuable. The pain is temporary, and feeling and acting different is very normal for bereavement. Think of yourself in bed with the flu. You *know* that in time your temperature will drop and you will be back to normal, but while you are aching and your teeth are chattering, it is hard to believe that within hours you will feel much better. It is like that when you are in a state of bereavement, or bereaved. You are so miserable inside that you cannot believe that things will ever be different. They will, but sometimes it can take quite a while.

Specialists in bereavement, called thanatologists, say that the pain is really part of the healing. A scar on your body may hurt before it fades and heals, but that discomfort actually shows that mending is going on. So it is with the emotional scars of bereavement. The pain is normal and shows that healing is taking place. After a long time it goes away, leaving only a hint of the former hurt.

"This Can't Be Happening to Me"

Right after someone you love dies, you are bound to be shocked. "It can't be," you say. You keep expecting the death to be a bad dream, hoping you'll awaken to find things as before. During the initial weeks, you are so taken aback that you scarcely seem to be functioning. When you dress, do school work, or converse, you're merely going through the motions. Your mind is elsewhere. Your numb body barely manages the daily tasks of living. For example, at 7:00 P.M. you might scrub the tub with scouring powder, but then completely neglect to rinse it, remembering only when your sister complains the next morning about the grit in the tub.

Accompanying your numbness is the beginning of your deep sadness. Tears may pour out, as your body reacts to what your mind has been told. You may complain you have no stamina and are fatigued, yet sleep may not come. Or you may sleep for what seems an endless number of hours. Interest in food may disappear. Parts of your body may ache or bother you. Dry throats are common, as is shortness of breath. A new and odd fragility may overwhelm you: could you break as easily as a bone china teacup?

Watching changes in your body and mind is startling enough. A week or two after the death you think you've been through more than you can stand. You can't get the person out of your mind. However, your grief is only beginning. It is far from complete, with painful reactions to come that will help you adjust to the new you.

Your feelings are so intense because, after someone close to you dies, you lose part of yourself. The world, as you have known it, has been irreparably altered; it may seem to have fallen to pieces. Because you must re-create your world and put yourself together in it without the person you relied upon so heavily, the changes in you will be massive. In a sense, you must form a new identity.

Doing the work to get put together again takes a long

time. The hardest labor is not done during the first shock of death but after that blow is met. The well-known author Madeleine L'Engle expressed it best when she said that grief is like a deep cut—it doesn't hurt until the numbness wears off.

What are some of the directions your hurt will take?

The Table Is Set, but No One Comes

Very likely one of your first reactions is to disbelieve and test the reality of your loss. Perhaps you long for things to be as they were so badly that you pretend the person is still around. You listen for familiar footsteps or accidentally set a place at the table. You even catch yourself planning things to say the next time you meet.

You test again and again. The dead person turns up in your dreams. Perhaps in the dream's story you valiantly run to the authorities who decide such matters, in hopes of saving the person from dying. You awaken to reality, shattered that the death can't be undone.

As part of denying the reality of loss, people of all ages sometimes try to strike up a bargain—with themselves, with fate, with God. The bargain goes like this: If I will be especially good or sacrificing, will you please return my loved one to me? It might mean dieting or fasting, going overboard with mannerly consideration and helpfulness, or doing the best job ever in school or career. Whatever the form, the bargain must be tested and proven false.

The only danger in these bargains is that some people are so disappointed when their magic fails that they take the pendulum in the opposite direction. As though trying to make up for time lost in martyrdom, they then gorge themselves, create havoc, or quit school or work. If something like this is happening to you, perhaps you can identify the bargain, doomed from the start, which you tried to strike.

Many people also report feeling that their deceased loved one lurks near, watching and judging their actions. Such sensations can make survivors frightened and uneasy. Some even wonder if they are going crazy.

When things like this happen, it does not show mental illness, but only that survivors are clinging to their loved ones, trying to make them return by denying the truth. It is calming just to know that this and other forms of denial are quite common. They fade once you can "say good-bye" to the person's support in your life.

Anger Turns Outward

Protest against the death you must face shows up in other forms besides denial. One of these is anger. Most people who mourn feel angry toward the dead person. If you're angry, you may have good reason.

Perhaps the person ignored health warnings and viewed visits to a doctor as a sign of weakness, staying away until it was too late. Perhaps the person was careless with safety matters and death could easily have been prevented. Or perhaps elaborate scenarios were played out to "protect the children," leaving you out of significant family discussions and decisions. These events cannot be changed. As a result, you feel pain and rage.

One of the reasons you're angry, even if your relative or friend did everything possible to stay alive, is that life is not within your control. You have been cheated. "Why me?" you ask. "Now I'll never have a mother (father, brother, sister, grandparent, aunt, uncle, special friend, etc.)." As if life were a drama, you go over the roles that person played in your life and recognize that these roles now go unfilled. If your uncle played checkers with you often, it's likely you are playing checkers less now. If your father picked you up in his car after school, it's possible you're busing home now. You keenly respond to all the voids, identifying all the ramifications of your loss.

Very often it's something small that you miss, but it saddens and angers you deeply anyway. Harry Warden felt this way. Orphaned after an auto accident, his uncle Gordon and aunt Dot took fine care of him and tried to ease his grief. He appreciated their efforts but was lonely.

Because his aunt and uncle had not lived with Harry for the twelve years before he came to them, they just couldn't know everything he had shared with his parents. Nor could they know that much about Harry's habits—what he liked, what he disliked, what would make him comfortable.

Harry soon noticed that in his new home, no one ever brought him a present without an occasion. Harry missed his parents' wonderful way of surprising him with small gifts they claimed bore his name. Once it was an especially hard jigsaw puzzle. Another time he received a book of poems about the sea. This wasn't his foster parents' style. Harry's anger and sadness intensified when he realized Gordon and Dot wouldn't even know what to get him if it were.

Anger can be let out in several ways. It is often focused at others. Some are blameworthy, others are not. You may be incensed at those who sadly attended the funeral but then hastily forgot the dead person (and you) to go about having fun, while you continue to suffer. You may be angry with other survivors, for reasons unclear even to you, with explosive irritability the result. Perhaps you're angry with them simply for being survivors. And you may be angry at God, for doing such an unexpected, cruel thing to you. It's normal to feel anger toward others and important to realize why.

Anger Turns Inward

Your anger can be turned inward, toward yourself as well. One of the reasons people become angry with themselves in bereavement is because of guilt or feelings of remorse for offenses real and imagined. If you are like most people, being angry at the defenseless dead makes you wonder what kind of person *you* are. You might decide that you must be rather nasty.

Your guilt may stem from the times in life you'd wished the person would disappear off the face of the earth. Fran Higgins's little sister Erica had a talent for finding Fran's property, no matter how carefully hidden from view. She seemed to use her auburn pigtails as radar. Once found, however, Erica never returned the object to its place in working condition. How often Fran wanted to strangle her incorrigible pest of a sister! After Erica's death from leukemia, it was difficult for Fran to keep the truth in mind: that bad thoughts and wishes exert absolutely no influence upon actual events. The notion that a part of life is given over to chance and luck is not always within people's philosophies.

Death embarrasses many people. Often they don't know how to tell others of a death that has affected them; nor do they know how to receive the news. Awkwardness makes them wonder why they are humiliated. They've done nothing wrong and they know it. But when they can't answer their own questions, guilt can be the result.

Guilt can also result from business that remained unfinished at the time of death. During his early teen years, Stephen lumbered about his home, rudely demonstrating boredom and impatience with other members of the household. He was disgusted by his accountant father's eagerness for job security, revolted by his mother's craving for success in her children, and infuriated by his brother's interest in loud music. From the pedestal that Stephen had created for himself, he could look down on everything and everyone around him. Just when his conceit and disdain were at their worst, Stephen's mother died suddenly. "Now I'll never have a chance to tell her how I really felt deep down inside," Stephen says. "I knew she cared for all of us and I gave her such a hard time."

Guilt can also arise if you are glad someone close to you has died. This is not as strange or uncommon as it might sound. When a family member has been terminally ill for a long time, it hurts everyone to watch that person linger on without peace or dignity. There is relief when death finally occurs. There is also relief when a relationship that has been characterized by intolerable rancor or brutality comes to an end. Those who are seriously abused physically or mentally by someone close take genuine comfort that the force of destruction is gone. People rarely mention it aloud if they are glad someone has died. Most are sure they're alone in this response. As a result, they are likely to feel small and nasty, when actually it's quite natural to welcome the end of anything that has been unbearable.

Why Was I Left?
With death, survivors sometimes feel that they have been rejected. Mildred reacted this way, wondering if her dead aunt had loved her. "If she did," Mildred thought, "how could she have deserted me this way. Did she punish me for the bad things I said?" Bob put it another way. Speaking of his grandmother's death, he said bluntly, "Grandma died on me."

Young people are not alone in such attitudes. Adults also feel bereft; they, too, feel guilty for blaming the dead person for their abandonment. Adults merely cover this emotion better than young people do. Neither youngsters nor their elders should try to hide their rejection. It is normal.

Fear Goes Along with Death
Rejection is often coupled with fear. We fear our own eventual deaths. We fear the future deaths of others.

And sometimes we fear grieving or watching the ones we love grieve.

From the moment we realize that life must end, until we actually die, the thought of death remains in the back of our minds. Look at your life. Have thoughts about death returned now and then? Have they been sparked by specific incidents—the death of someone you know, reports of deaths on the news? You can expect your mind to turn to death as you go on with the business of life. These are natural thoughts, which should not be shut off. Only by allowing your mind to explore and by asking questions can you grow comfortable with the concept that extinction is a natural event, not a punishment.

In the months after someone close to them dies, many people fear their own deaths, vividly conjuring up the circumstances under which it might occur and sometimes developing symptoms of illness. Your aches can be caused by the lifelessness of grief. Without joy or vigor, you may compare yourself to your dead loved one, feeling and acting half dead.

Besides fearing their own deaths, many bereaved people are anxious about the survival of their parents or other loved ones. Perhaps this is happening to you. No doubt it puts a real scare into you, making you feel uneasy. The question that underlies your discomfort (and which can indeed be put into words) is "Who will take care of me?" If you share your questions about abandonment and death, you learn that young people are not alone in fear of being without support. Most adults also want companionship and someone to care for them.

Emotions are not simple, though. You can want companionship one moment and spurn it the next. The mind is funny. Take a look at one girl's thoughts. When she was about ten, Robin's parents decided she was responsible enough to be left alone in the house for short evening periods. While she reveled in her new maturity, at about the time her parents were expected to return, Robin repeatedly imagined their ghastly deaths in an auto accident. How sorry everyone would feel for her! What attention she would enjoy! Alarmed by the fact that she'd killed her parents off in a fantasy, Robin covered her shame by praying for their safe return. Somehow, prayers didn't make her daydreams disappear, and they continue to pop up to this day.

After worrying about it for two years, Robin got up the nerve to mention it to her friend Sara. Sara had heard that most young people invent either their own deaths or those of their parents, sometimes fashioning fictional scripts for complete funerals within their minds.

By envisioning deaths in this way, young people succeed in frightening themselves. They also manage to reassure themselves that they can indeed cope with whatever life may hold.

Depression

When the truth of a real death registers, the sadness and longing a person feels in bereavement may be overwhelming. One can become so dull, gloomy, helpless, and drained of emotion that all that seems to be left is utter emptiness and isolation. The person might like to be up, but everything points down. Doctors call this state of being depression, It is a justifiable response to reality. Depression will usually decrease as the bereaved person does the work of mourning.

When you have been through a death experience, you may feel some of the emotions described here: shock, denial, anger, guilt, fear of abandonment, fear of death, sadness, and depression. Or you may feel other things. What sums it up best is to say that during bereavement it is normal to feel and act different from the way you usually do. Change is normal.

Absent and Delayed Mourning

What is most important is to express whatever it is you do feel. The expression of grief emotion is called mourning; it is the act of working through the pain. Many young people don't let their families or friends in on their grief, choosing instead to suffer in silence alone. Some try to make it appear they have no grief at all. Hilary Benton is like that.

Last summer when Hilary was fifteen, her father died. A month later, in September, Hilary's friend Lisa returned from vacation and asked about Hilary's father, who had been ill. "Oh, he died," replied Hilary, with the strength and emotion she would apply in announcing she'd just eaten a hamburger.

Hilary's mourning appears to be absent or at least delayed. If Hilary is allowed to continue to respond in this manner, she might eventually succeed in shutting off all feeling concerning her tragedy. She will inhibit the normal progression of mourning. Because she cannot cope with the idea of death, she will try to put off accepting the final reality of her loss.

Perhaps Hilary will be lucky and will expulse her grief at a later date. Sometimes emotion is expressed on an anniversary of the death. Sometimes it begins at the time of a second meaningful death.

Until Hilary can allow the finality of death into her life, she might not be truly capable of going on with the joys of living. She'll always be battling with her mourning, unsuccessfully campaigning against a pervasive sadness she can't explain.

If mourning remains absent or delayed for many years, it can get in the way of adult relationships. Never having told anyone how deserted she felt, Hilary may remain fearful of repeated rejection and abandonment. As a result, she may not be able to give fully to marriage and children.

"I'm Only Sad for a Little While"

Perhaps you do not hide and cover your grief as carefully as Hilary does. Perhaps, instead, you can express your reactions for awhile, but then quickly replace your distress with industrious, happy pursuits. You might construct models, ride a bicycle, go to parties, or have a joke session with friends.

You wonder how you can be overcome by grief one moment and absorbed or actually jubilant the next. Your relatives may be confounded as well. They may even criticize you: "Where is your respect? Didn't you love—?

What will the neighbors say when they see you out cavorting?"

This kind of expression, which seems to turn itself on and off, is *not* delayed mourning. It is *not* absent mourning. It is *not* a danger signal that places your future emotional development in jeopardy.

In fact, on-again-off-again mourning is very normal for young people; it should not be discouraged, even though it sometimes resembles lack of feeling. It is called the "short sadness span."

If you go through this, you do feel, and you feel quite intensely. Your emotions are so profound, however, that it would seem intolerable to continue exploring them all at once. Dr. Martha Wolfenstein, who investigated and named the "short sadness span", concluded that young people were terrified at being at the mercy of their own grief. One of the youngsters in her study group was asked what would happen if youngsters let out all their feelings. He responded, "They would cry and cry. They would cry for a month and not forget it. They would cry every night and dream about it, and the tears would roll down their eyes and they wouldn't know it. And they would be thinking about it and tears just running down their eyes at night while they were dreaming."

It is understandable if you're reluctant to let go all at once, for you have spent much of your growing time in life learning to maintain control. It is understandable if you must become preoccupied with devoting much of your energy to everyday living.

4

You Can Handle Your Feelings

You can handle your feelings after death has hit you. You are able to deal with them because you are not a newcomer to coping with separation. You've managed other loss experiences: moving, losing a treasured memento or piece of jewelry, bearing it as a friend seeks out others instead of you. These were all loss situations in which you mourned when separated from people and things you loved. Coping with these smaller happenings in life has prepared you to deal with a major bereavement.

Successful bereavement after a death is achieved only when a bereaved person is able to do the work of mourning. After the grief has spilled forth, a new pattern of living takes hold. The dead person can no longer be depended upon. This is similar to what had to be done before in other loss situations. Your losses were accepted, not forgotten. If you moved, you slowly got used to being without the conveniences of your old locale. If you lost a necklace, you caught yourself trying to wear it on special occasions and felt its absence. If a friend abandoned you, there were many lonely Saturdays.

Perhaps you eventually filled your emptiness when substitutes were found—a new shopping center, library, and park to replace the old; another beloved ornament; and a new friend to pal around with. But perhaps you did not. In any case, after losing a part of your world, your return to wholeness involved a mourning process. Following the death of someone close, the mourning process resembles what you have been through in other losses. The difference is one of degree, not kind. After death, mourning is more painful. The ache crouches deep within your being; letting it out is part of a healing procedure that restores calm and order.

Grief can be very powerful. It can knock you over to feel so much wishing or sadness or anger or shame. Imagine yourself standing up to your waist in the ocean, totally unprepared for each wave that comes along. You fall down in surprise. It's difficult to get completely up to your feet again because, before you know it, another wave comes along to knock you down again. You can think of grief as being a set of waves, each one capable of sending you reeling.

Now imagine yourself in the ocean again, up to your waist, only this time you are mentally and physically prepared to take on each new wave. The result is that you are challenged, remain on your feet, and possibly even find the ocean a source of exhilaration. Mourning for a dead person or pet will probably never be called exhilarating. But in successful mourning, you slowly ride the waves of grief and bring them under control. To quote Earl Grollman, a noted rabbi-thanatologist, "Mourning is the process that guarantees that we happen to our grief rather than having our grief happen to us."

This chapter will present a scrapbook of ideas that might aid you in doing your mourning work. Some of the information and suggestions will apply to you, some will not. Take from the chapter what *you* need to help you handle your feelings. Think about it: You are eager to cope—just picking up this book and getting this far shows you are ready.

For a beginning consider the idea of having your parent or another adult you trust read this book. Sharing your reactions to these proposals could inspire other ideas.

Reality Must be Tested

Death is shocking. Some feel they are falling to pieces. Watch your body reactions. You might record the changes in yourself on a chart. Are there certain times of the day, week, or month when you feel particularly down? Or peculiar? Or unable to function well?

Jacob's best friend Lance died when they were both in sixth grade. Knowing that death was permanent, he claimed acceptance of Lance's death. Nevertheless, each time he met Lance's family in the neighborhood or saw Lance's sister in school, he couldn't eat for several days afterward and suffered painful stomachaches. Does anything like this happen to you? Can you identify the events that trigger reactions in your body? Pinning down specific reasons for somatic changes can be a first step in working through feelings. Talk about the funny things your body is doing, again and again. Don't worry about boring others. Repeating your stories will blunt the edge of your pain and bring you closer to accepting the death.

Jacob was uncomfortable when he saw Lance's family because part of him wanted to pretend Lance was not dead, but merely away for a while. Seeing them would jar Jacob and keep him from one-sided conversations he was holding with the buddy who couldn't answer. Jacob was denying the reality of Lance's death because he wasn't ready to say good-bye to a wonderful friendship. Jacob needed Lance by his side, and so, by magic, he conjured him to be there. It would be helpful for Jacob, and it might be helpful to you, to know that denial fades once you have tested reality sufficiently. Once you have met up with enough instances in which the necessary individual cannot help you meet your needs, you simply *must* accept the reality of the loss. This will happen to Jacob after he meets Lance's family many, many times, and after he becomes adjusted to going to the movies, the store, and school without him. It will happen faster if Jacob resists the temptation to avoid Lance's family and takes the time to speak with them instead, admitting that much has changed in his life.

When reality has been tested countless painful times, a bereaved person becomes ready to do without the deceased person's support. When that happens to you, the dead person will not hang around your shoulder. Rather, when you form an image of him or her, the figure is likely to be standing further away, perhaps in a nearby hallway or down the street. At that point, even if you try with all your might, you may not be able to get the imagined presence to place itself closer to you.

It has been said that if all your relationships were considered to exist in a house, once the denial of bereavement faded, then the deceased person and everything associated with that person would be in a room with a closed door. The door would then have to be consciously opened in order to partake of the relationship once shared. This would be a new kind of sharing, for of necessity it is a one-way relationship.

When you imagine the dead person further from yourself, it's a sign you have been successfully climbing the steps of mourning. Look for this change or something like it. Remember one thing, however. Death is forever. For the rest of your life, the death will affect you, so don't be dismayed if, years after you have done the initial testing, an unexpected episode of denial leaves you feeling raw inside.

At the author's wedding, eight years after her father had died, she found herself wandering from room to room in the reception hall. Puzzled by her aimlessness, she suddenly realized the meandering was a search for her father, as if she expected him to be present on such an important occasion. This is an example of denial long after the actual death.

Death Is Frustrating

Thinking about what is not to be yours inevitably leads to anger. Anger is fine, as long as you can accept it, use it as a tool to get yourself other things which *can* be had, and do not let it eat at you.

In feeling love for others, it is a sad fact that everyone does not always live happily ever after. However, a crucial aspect of succeeding as a human being is continuing to maintain the capacity for allowing yourself to have feelings for others. Philosopher Bertrand Russell said it this way: "To fear love is to fear life, and those who fear life are already three parts dead." To be truly open for further love, psychologists say you must be able to allow *all* feelings, not just happiness and love, to surface.

Some young people push their anger deep beneath the surface. Perhaps because at an earlier date they were told dead angels are listening in on their thoughts. As they imagine rage might not meet with the approval of deities, they try to make such feelings disappear. Some families intensify fear of the dead by telling children the dead person is ashamed of their misdeeds. If this happens in your family, tell people how you feel about it.

Express your anger. Let it out with your body. You can hit a punching bag, hammer on wood, or tear cloth. You might play a hard game of ball, ride a fierce bicycle, walk very fast, or throw pillows back and forth with someone.

Talk about your anger, and don't try to put it out of your mind. Think about it, for that is the only way you will ever be rid of it. On the television show "M*A*S*H," one of the characters, named Radar, said that in adolescence he'd been angry with his father for dying. His anger ceased only when he recognized that it wasn't his father's idea to go and die. Had Radar not allowed his mind to turn to unpleasant thoughts, he never would have reached his comforting conclusion.

Talking about anger can do more than alter thoughts: It can alter events, as seen in Diane Alsworth's case. Diane was in seventh grade when her mother died. Suddenly the house became so quiet, so empty. The hours between school dismissal and her father's arrival from work in the city seemed endless. The thirty minute drive from Chicago to Diane's suburb appeared longer than it ever had before. And pretty soon, Diane's father was spending more and more evenings away from Diane and her sister. To forget his own sorrow, he was letting office matters engulf him. By the time he'd leave his office and drive home, Diane would often be either in bed or too angry to see him. One Wednesday night, he found the door double-bolted upon his arrival. His fumbling attempts to enter the house through windows were to no avail. And Diane would answer his banging on the door only with hysterical cries: "You don't care about us." In a few minutes, Diane calmed down and let her father in. Diane, her father, and her sister sat down to talk.

There are times when talk about angry feelings starts off calmly; at other times, emotional outburst precedes discussion of issues. While rational approaches may be more desirable, through his daughter's lock-out, Diane's father did learn. Realizing that she needed the one parent she had left, he agreed to make every effort to be home most nights.

You Are Not to Blame

In some cases, guilt becomes so great that a young person will seek punishment in order to be rid of blame. Carol's young cousin died in a fire. Very upset, Carol began shoplifting. When she was finally caught, she seemed glad, as though a burden had been lifted from her shoulders. Carol felt she had paid her dues. Now she could go back to the business of living after her cousin had died.

Talk about your guilt so you can set it aside.

The More You Know, the Better You'll Feel

Death brings out so many fears in us. If you fear you will be alone, talk over your fears as specifically as you can. Urge your surviving relatives to have thorough physical examinations. Have one yourself. It will help to allay your worst suspicions.

Your concern over who will care for you in the event of your parents' deaths is a legitimate one. It's a good idea for a parent to provide for the remote possibility of disaster by having a will drawn up. The directions in the will insure that young people are not left without guardians. Ask your parent (or foster parent) about his or her will. Find out if someone has been chosen to see to your financial security and if that person has agreed to the arrangement. If no one has been chosen, talk to your parent about the wisdom of selecting someone.

Find out even more. Find out what plans have been made for your education. Ask your parents if they carry out a yearly review of finances, so that poor last minute choices need not be made. Think about the person who would care for you if you *were* left alone. Do you like that person? Is the guardian someone you could adjust to living with? Would that person create emotional warmth for you, as well as financial security? If not, can you have a say? The more you know about your future, the better you'll feel.

You may find that you are already designing life without your parents when there's been no actual tragedy. Instead of letting the fantasy deaths you concoct worry you, consider accepting them as part of normal thought and feeling. Acceptance may come more easily if you examine stories that deal with horror and death. The grim terror found in good literature can help you come to terms with this aspect of the human condition. In a magazine interview, writer Ray Bradbury had this to say when asked if his collection of violent stories called *Dark Carnival* could help people:

> [Those stories] are helping us to accept our fantasies so that we won't feel guilty about them. We all have lists of people we would like to kill, starting when we were children, when the first competition comes into the family. When I was six and my sister was born, I was displaced and wished her dead. The next thing I knew, she was. She died of pneumonia when I was seven. A child may not even know that he remembers wanting that competition dead . . . and then God very conveniently provides bacteria and gets rid of the competition, and you

triumph. For a little while you say, "Hey, wow! She's gone!" Then you suddenly remember that she's not coming back *ever*, and it hurts and you have mixed feelings of sorrow and guilt; who knows how deeply these feelings run? The purpose, then, of a *good* horror story is to exorcise these demons; is to bring them out and say, "Look, you're no different than anyone else." We've all had these feelings about our brothers, our sisters, our mothers and fathers. . . . They were invented by the Greeks and they must have thought about them before they wrote them down. . . .

So, a good horror story takes that raw material and says, "OK, everyone, we're gonna have a real gangbusting time tonight! We're gonna break open the top of your skull and show you that you have a skeleton inside your body or that you *wanted* to kill your father or your sister or your best friend!" I remember when I was twelve, there was a boy in junior high school with me who was beautiful. He ran as swift as the wind. One day he stepped on a nail and had to have his foot cut off, and all of us boys celebrated. You see, that's *grim*. That's a terrible *truth* to face up to. But that's what all the old fairy tales, the really good ones, are about.

Pain Shows That You're Alive

With death often comes sadness and depression. Believe it or not, the sharp pain really shows how you are growing as a person. If you were less, you would not be able to react in this way to the end of a relationship. Allow your humanness to flow. Don't try to turn off or delay this expression of being alive.

There may be unexpected moments when you suddenly weep. It might be in reaction to losing a small possession, such as a hat. Or a dramatic movie might touch you and offer an excuse to cry. These are probably really moments of mourning. Minor events can trigger your pervading sadness, bringing it to the surface. Try to recognize your mourning even when it disguises itself. Whatever cloak it wears, let yourself mourn in response. If you don't, gloom may hover over you for much longer than necessary.

Time Does Heal Wounds

Hopelessness and helplessness fade when certain events take place. First, time must pass. How hard it is for people in contemporary western society to allow time to do its work! With our fast foods and instant-on television sets, we let our preference for immediate gratification be known.

Despite technology, the loss of a loved one is a situation that will heal only in its own time. No one can direct a bereaved person to a quick service booth where mourning might be condensed. We all wish there were such a kiosk. Instead, perhaps the first step toward alleviating the sadness might be to accept the fact that the ache of bereavement fades *only* with the passage of time. This has been proven informally by generations and formally by today's thanatologists. Try to remember it will be better next year.

While mourning requires time, you can do more than wait in your room crossing off weeks on a calendar. You can facilitate your healing.

Share Memories

Sadness decreases if you simply talk about the dead person in all aspects. Charlotte Zolotow's picture book, *My Grandson Lew,* touches many ages because its characters, mother and son, open up about the grandfather they both miss. For four years young Lewis has not even been told about the man's death. He has waited for his grandfather to return, it seems. When he finally inquires, his questions enable his mother to share with him. At the close, Lew says, "I miss him." Lew's mother responds, "So do I. . . . But now we will remember him together and neither of us will be so lonely as we would be if we had to remember him alone."

Death has come to picture books only recently, but advice for coping with grief is found in much of the history of literature. Two Biblical quotations are particularly appropriate here: "Weep with those who weep" is from Romans (12:15); and from Proverbs (23:18), "Surely there is a future and thy hope wilt not be cut off."

The future will indeed come, and it will be helped along if those with whom you share your memories truly listen. Whether you choose to speak with an adult or another young person, be wary of those who are interested but will not permit you to express yourself in the way that is natural for you. People who announce, "Men mustn't cry" or "Pull yourself together and get on with it" are not showing empathy. They may try to sympathize, but instead they impose their own standards for feelings and behavior.

If they can't accept the fact that what is natural for you is what may be right for you (even if that means you are not sad); if they cannot allow you to be what you must be, try telling them how their response affects you. If they still can't control their urges to alter your thoughts, consider finding others with whom you can share on a genuine basis.

If you do find someone who will truly listen, try your hardest to talk. If words will not leave your mouth, write to your listener.

But sometimes there is no listener for either words or letter. Your chance to unburden yourself may come when someone else you know has a death experience and wants to share it with you. If you spontaneously want to tell about your own reactions and don't insist that your friend's be the same, seize the opportunity to let yourself go.

In writing this book, the author was expressing her need to let out thoughts and feelings about bereavement. Find your way. If there is no audience to write to, address yourself. Write a journal, or a poem. Your expression need not be limited to verbal form. Perhaps you will find painting a form of release, or dance, or filmmaking. Form is not as important as finding a way to let yourself—and possibly others—know what is inside.

Time Alone Is Also Valuable

Sharing is helpful for the relief of your sadness, but a certain amount of solitude is necessary, too. Some people madly rush around to escape their feeling of aloneness.

It's understandable that there will be times during bereavement when it may panic you to be alone—during a holiday, for example. At those times, be sure adults and young people you like surround you in life-supporting activities. But try not to overschedule your days. Take time to be with yourself.

Time alone will help you know how you're feeling. In your room or on a walk you may unpop the cork on some of the emotions you've kept in. In privacy, it may be easier to cry, to go back over the old days, to pray, to strike out in anger.

In your room or on a walk, you can look around at the world. The petals of a flower, the formation of the clouds, the crisscross patterns of your skin: These, and more, remind you of the beauty of the universe of which you are a part. Examining your surroundings, you may come to realize that each seemingly small person, animal, and object plays a very important role in earth's ecology. Year after year, as you watch the flowers return in the spring, you may come to a peaceful sense of the continuity of life. If time is not set aside for solitude, the hubbub of daily existence can camouflage the wonder of life.

Another solitary avenue for coping with feelings is through reading. Books have been tools for preventing and solving problems for as long as both the books and the problems have existed. The door of the library at ancient Thebes bore the inscription, "Healing place of the soul." The values of reading fiction and nonfiction are many.

Reading offers an opportunity to identify with others

like yourself. If you read about a youngster your age who has also lost someone close, you will involve yourself in a character's attempt to face life's challenges. Do you see yourself as an unwilling victim in a drama you cannot control? Does hopelessness permeate your being? Do you wonder if love can transcend death? If you're going through these things, you will find characters who also respond to these themes. Within the privacy of your mind, without observation or interference, you can get an idea of how one protagonist copes. You might then rehearse potential solutions to your own dilemmas. "Read to weigh and consider," said Francis Bacon.

In reading about loss, you may reach the conclusion that you are not alone. A literary personage, one who's quite normal in fact, shares your situation. With such figures for company, you can relive episodes in your life and relieve yourself of the emotions that drag you down.

Finally, after being part of the experiences of a literary character, you just might be able to talk with another human being about some of your own. And then, in a spirit of comfortable reciprocity, those human beings might disclose their thoughts and feelings to you. In listening, it might surprise you to find that these real people have problems similar to yours. Your discovery could lead the two of you to search out real solutions together.

Books don't promise any or all of these things. In fact, sometimes the mirror of your own emotions may prove unbearable. I was told the story of a wheelchair-bound teenager who had become paralyzed in a diving accident. While still bereaved over loss of the use of her legs, she was looking over Pamela Walker's book, *Twyla*. She asked the school librarian, "Is it realistic?" When the response was yes, she declined the book. "No, thanks," she said. "I have my own realism."

You, too, may want to stay far away from literary themes of loss right now. Your friends, who have not yet grieved, may read those very books with great interest, subsequently developing understanding of your feelings. This, in turn, will increase your comfort with one another. For them, reading is also an opportunity to prepare vicariously for their own eventual losses.

No matter who is doing the reading, devouring scores of books will never amount to a pill you can take to replace the labor needed for answering the tough questions of bereavement. They can be part of the effort, though.

The Place of Therapy

All people need and can use the support of family and friends during bereavement. Some people need even more. Because loss overwhelms them, they can benefit from the services of a professional therapist. A therapist can be a psychiatrist who is a medical doctor, a psychologist, a social worker, a trained member of the clergy or a counselor. Such people are taught to be of help to individuals with persistent or seemingly overwhelming difficulties. After going to school and getting experience on the job, a therapist should know a good deal about loss and how people adjust to it. A therapist offers a place to talk over problems, creating a setting where a person is encouraged to feel free enough to discuss feelings and events never before divulged. The therapist sees people individually or in groups. With a good therapist, the person who has come for help is led toward insight and understanding. The person can then work toward a happier life.

You can seek therapy privately or through social agencies in your community. Some agencies have begun therapy groups with a particular bent—realizing the profound impact of family loss, they have put together groups consisting exclusively of young people who have lost a family member. With the therapist's help, they express and examine their feelings. Youngsters in such groups are surprised to find that their thoughts are quite normal. They eventually come to better terms with both their emotions and themselves. Possible locations for such groups include the "Y," a church, synagogue, mental health center, medical clinic, school, or welfare center.

You might be interested in exploring your community to see if such a group exists or might be started. If you cannot find out yourself, perhaps a parent, teacher, or a member of the clergy can. Ask your questions in a direct way, so that the person trying to help you knows what you want. If you can't ask for help aloud, write your request.

Whether it is individual or group therapy you seek, the location is not as important as the presence of a leader who is sensitive and educated concerning psychology and problems of loss. Some of the organizations listed in the Appendix might serve as resources for finding such a person. Nearby medical schools, medical school-affiliated hospitals, and schools of social work also try to offer satisfactory referrals.

Once referred to an individual, look into that person's professional training. An M.D. can be checked in the *American Medical Directory,* a reference book found in most libraries. Licensed psychologists are listed in the *Biographical Directory* of the American Psychological Association.

If you cannot find a listing for your therapist in established reference sources, do not hesitate to ask that person for credentials and a history of past and current professional affiliations. Make sure you are not getting involved with an incompetent quack who has decided to hang out a shingle.

If you have not been able to locate an individual of reputation on your own, think about the option of working through a neighborhood social agency or large medical partnership, one which has been established for awhile. In such groups, professionals screen each other and standards are likely to be maintained.

In your first interview, look for signs that you will be in good hands. You can expect a fairly orderly office, and the first session should be one in which you are made to feel at ease. At the same time, the therapist should be able to get a basic idea about you, your family, your ideas, and your problems.

Individual or group therapy that is well conducted should be helpful to everyone. Some people value it so highly they consider it a requisite of healthful living, the way play is for youngsters and meaningful work is for adults. They wish everyone would take part.

Desire to alleviate the pain of bereavement is just cause for seeking help. Certain bereavement problems are more serious than others, of course, but if you fit into any of the categories listed below, please give some thought to the possible benefits of therapy in your life.

Think about therapy if—

- you are continually bored or uninterested.

- it is months after the death and your body is still reacting strongly to bereavement (you cannot sleep or eat, and you feel continuously ill).

- you cannot talk about the dead person at all and cannot bear mention of your loss.

- you have shed no tears at all since the death.

- information about the death was withheld from you for a considerable period.

- you frequently assault others or threaten to do so.

- you are deeply unhappy about being a boy or girl.

- you physically abuse or torture your pets.

- you are afraid to move your bowels.

- you frequently think of killing yourself.

- you are desperately frightened to go to school.

- you are unable to do school work or concentrate.

- you are continually in a state of panic.
- you have suddenly begun to set fires, shoplift, or participate in other serious delinquent acts.
- you have begun to become heavily involved in the drug scene.
- you got along very poorly with a dead parent.
- you get along very poorly with the surviving parent.
- the surviving parent wants you to sleep in his or her bed.
- you are being asked to take over for a dead parent.
- suicide was the cause of a parent's death.

In this chapter, many suggestions have been offered. They all try to convey one central message: Go through your mourning.

Work at your mourning; climb its steps. Test reality again and again until you believe and accept the death. Go over your memories, good and bad. If your mourning span has to be short, make sure to leave opportunities to return to it again and again. Allowing mourning to take place is the healthiest way to detach yourself from the person who has died. Only then can you restructure your life.

5

When Someone Special Dies

Each death is different. Each has its unique effect upon you. News on television of the death of a famed politician, athlete, or movie star affects you in one way. You may be sad. Your sadness will be for the world, as well as yourself, because the universe will be forever altered. Hearing that a friend's father has died affects you in quite another way. You may be sad for your friend, while feeling fearful and relieved for yourself.

These deaths enter your thoughts and influence the way you view life, but they still are not part of your inner being. The intensity of your mourning passes quickly without requiring much adjustment on your part.

It is obvious that your bereavement lasts much longer when someone much closer dies. It is not so readily apparent, though, that each special death requires its own adjustment, which depends upon the relationship you had with the one who died.

The Death of a Pet

A pet's death is an important event in your life; human beings establish deeply personal bonds with their pets. Perhaps you know people who truly think of their pets as members of the family; perhaps such people are to be found in your home. For some people, the bonds are so strong they choose to lie next to their pets in death. This is not silly. President Franklin Roosevelt is buried next to his beloved dog Fala in Hyde Park.

The death of your pet may serve as your first taste of death. The word "serve" is an appropriate one because the unfortunate experience actually aids growth. You are deeply upset and undergo many of the emotions discussed in Chapter 3. But in going through the anger, guilt, loneliness, and other emotions, you have a chance to learn about life and death. It is said that you have a dress rehearsal for other losses.

The way in which you and your family handle such a practice session can strengthen you so that later deaths will be less shocking. Many families conduct mock funerals for pets. This is a fine idea because it allows everyone to exhibit emotion without shame, to invent rituals, and to play and sing in memory of the animal. Some young people feel guilty when they spend more time playing than grieving, but the play really helps. In imitating what you think are actual funeral procedures, you calm yourself about the frightening unknown. Your pet's death gives you poise for later funeral attendance.

Perhaps you have been a part of extended "death"

games. You may have started them on the day of the pet's funeral, returning to them repeatedly. Part of the game may have been digging up the animal and examining it, or killing insects, burying them, and digging *them* up. If others found out about your "death" games, they may have been disgusted. If so, they probably let you know it. You may have been confused and ashamed.

"Death" games are not morbid, no matter how people react. They are a way to answer important questions: Where does my pet's body go? Does a pet have a soul? If I dream about my pet, will it come back? Is death really permanent?

Many parents rush to replace a dead pet. Hildy was surprised to find a new puppy in her house just the day after her dog Taba was killed by a car. Her parents were surprised, in turn, when Hildy greeted their generous act with rage. "Taba was special!" she shouted. "No dog will watch over me as well! No dog will stay at my side!"

Hildy tried to make her parents see that she *wanted* to cry for Taba, that they were making her uncomfortable about her tears. She was also hurt that they might think Taba, the solemn watchdog, was so easily replaceable.

Had Hildy's parents waited for her to shed her tears, she could then have begun to form a bond with a new dog. The affection would then have grown for the new dog's unique personality. She would not have tried to change the pup into a watchdog in the image of Taba. Hildy would have learned that love relationships are not interchangeable. She would also have found out that, after a time for mourning, life goes on.

The Death of a Friend

The death of a friend is deeply disturbing. So great is its force that your companion's face may haunt you for months, lingering indelibly in your mind's eye.

Of course, you always knew young people could die. You've watched television, read the papers, heard stories. But here it is for real. And you must acknowledge that if someone else your age can indeed die, so can you. That realization is part of the shock.

Your perturbed state may also be caused by the shame of it all: You are keenly aware of the struggles you and your friends have been through in past years. After gaining independence from parents ever so slowly, after managing to learn something about oneself, to be gone so soon is more than sad.

If your friend died of a terminal illness, it hurt you to watch as the self-reliance, which took so long to establish, had to be relinquished for hospital or bed care. And if part of your friend's face or body was disfigured, it bothered you. For you knew how deeply concerned and uncomfortable your friend was about physical appearance.

You are also upset because death has ended all promise. The growing years are given to dreams of heights to be reached. With life ended, any talents that might have been molded into mature reality are broken off. Your friend has no chance to create a future.

Inevitably, you turn back to face yourself and your own behavior. Questions must be asked: Were you a good friend? What sort of future are you molding? What if you were to die?

The sorrow of untimely loss is fair material for the creation of haunting memories.

The Death of a Grandparent, Uncle, or Aunt

The death of a grandparent, uncle, or aunt has special impact. These are members of your family—traditionally, their relationship to you is attentive and warm. Losing them is heartbreaking; family gatherings will never be the same.

Perhaps this is the first death you've encountered in your family. Perhaps this is also the first person you actually know who is dead. As such, this is your introduction to what mourning for a human being is all about. It's your first opportunity not only to mourn but to see how the adults around you respond to death.

These many factors mean that this death is very important: Your reactions and those of your family will affect the way you cope with other deaths. And there are as many ways to mourn as there are ways to be introduced to bereavement.

Some families find that awkwardness prohibits them from creating a calm and open atmosphere. With an aim to protect, they may delay telling of the death, whisking young people away during the funeral and formal condolence period. This makes death a whispered word. It discourages mourning. For these families, questions may be answered with misinformation, if not lies.

Take the case of Tricia Maddox, whose grandmother

died last year. Her parents told her, but it was clear they had many things to do, all of them without her. Before she could pack a bag, she was mysteriously driven to a friend's house. There she stayed three days, speaking to her parents only on the telephone. She later told her friend, another girl of thirteen, "When Mom and Dad picked me up, they pretended nothing had happened—that everything was just fine. I felt left out. Why did they give me the cold shoulder like that?"

Other families answer death in very different ways. They know intuitively that a relative's death hurts young people. They are aware how curious, confused, and shut out youngsters can be when it comes to death. In response, they create an atmosphere in which questions can be asked about funerals, cemeteries, and death itself. Facts and emotions are not hidden, and everyone attends the funeral and shares in the family's sadness. To be a member of one of these families means having a good start for coping with human death.

The Death of a Parent

Who would ever have thought a parent could die? If you were like most people, when you were younger you looked up and asked repeatedly, "When will you die?" Some parents foolishly promise, "I won't die until you're grown." Most are more realistic and advise, "Probably when I'm very old." What went wrong? Everything you know about the progress of medical science says it shouldn't have ended this way, and it shouldn't have ended now. That's one of the reasons you are so lonely.

There are other reasons, too. Psychiatrist Dr. John

Schowalter feels that you have lost not one, but two parents. One is lost because of death, while the other can no longer truly be with you because of mourning. Just as you are immersed in your bereavement and concentrate on little else, so is your surviving parent.

That parent must work through grief. It is common for a parent to become irritable, distant, inaccessible, or deeply depressed. In other words, all the things you are. It's easy to see that, in addition to your first loss, the parent who remains is not in a usual state. You can't help but become more insecure about your home life.

And there are so many changes to be insecure about.

Perhaps you fear losing a second time and experience panic whenever your surviving parent must leave for a long while. Maybe the situation has been further complicated: Has your mother only recently begun to work or your father changed jobs? Tell how you feel. For a short period, maybe the schedule can be modified or the number of trips minimized, giving you a chance to grow accustomed to your single-parent family. If not, perhaps you can make better arrangements for the times you are alone; your suggestions of whom you'd enjoy passing the hours with might be welcome.

Sometimes your mother or father's death is actually a predicament for you. It's very normal to be embarrassed about death, especially if you think you are utterly alone. In his autobiography, titled *Cavett,* Dick Cavett expressed his humiliation over his mother's death:

> I don't think I have ever recovered completely from my mother's death. She died of cancer when I was ten, and I still can't talk about it easily. I was in fifth grade at the

time, and having a dying mother was, aside from the sadness, an acute embarrassment to me. It sounds strange to say that, I know, but any kid who has been through it at such an age would know what I mean. Or would he? Some kids might enjoy the added attention, I suppose, but it killed me. I had the bad luck to be the only kid in my class, or that I had ever heard of, it seemed, who had such a thing happen to him, and it was excruciating. I already felt conspicuous because of my voice and my shortness and the loathsome fact that I was considered a "brain," and this added burden of sympathy was just too much.

. . . Maudlin sympathy angered and somehow shamed me, and whenever I overheard phrases like "poor little tyke" from supposedly well-meaning grownups I wished them incinerated on the spot.

Your embarrassment may be so great that you keep the death as secret as possible, which keeps you from finding out that others also live in single-parent families. Losing a parent through death happens to about one in six young people before they reach eighteen, so there clearly is company. In addition, a conservative survey indicates that approximately one marriage in three ends in divorce. That makes millions of young people who are victims of loss.

To cope with the awkwardness of losing a parent, many young people seek out others who also have only one parent. You may have noticed that before your mother or father died, most or all of your friends had two parents. Now you seem to be picking up youngsters from broken homes, one after another.

Is this something to worry about? Absolutely not. It might be happening because, right now, you are uncomfortable in homes with two parents. You miss the everyday events in such homes. It might hurt you to observe a married couple having a political discussion, something which is gone from your house, something you miss. Or pain might come as you watch another father or mother helping a friend with homework. For now, it may be that you can't bear to see happiness go unappreciated, taken for granted.

You may be choosing friends from single-parent homes because you sense their understanding. You may be living in a home where yelling has gotten out of hand, where a tirade can result if you leave an empty glass around. They may also be living that way.

In rage and frustration, your parent may blame you for things that can't possibly be your fault. This happened in the author's family after her father died. When my mother reached her boiling point with me, she would screech, "You broke his heart! *That's* what killed him!" It only happened two or three times, but I never forgot it, because a small part of me believed I'd really killed my father. Your friends from single-parent families may have to bear similar scapegoating during family bereavement.

While your surviving parent recognizes that major changes have taken place in the family, there may be worry about your sudden shift in friendships. Your parent may say more balance would do you good. Your mother or father probably realizes, however, that the adult company she or he has begun to keep has also seen a radical shift. Allow yourself to pursue the friends you want or need, no matter what their family constellations. Just as time will take care of your discomfort in two-parent homes, will diminish the yelling, and will cut down on scapegoating, so will it take care of balance in your friendships.

It is true that there are many hardships with only one parent. You have no alternate parent to turn to if your one parent is in a bad mood. But neither has your parent another adult to look to if *you* are acting up. What you do have is each other, any siblings, any friends, plus other adults. These people will be your company to weather the storm.

Some of your activities will change, some will not. Your surviving parent may not invite couples over as frequently. You may not like all of your parent's new single friends. Seeing them or hearing their voices on the phone may be enough to give you a stomachache. Their presence stabs you with reality of the profound differences in your life. Yet, other things will probably remain the same. Perhaps, in your house, leisurely Sunday breakfasts may continue to be as enjoyable as ever, a time which seems without change.

It's likely there will eventually be new people in your life, people who will add a new dimension to it. If you are lucky, there might be one adult with whom you develop a continuing relationship. If your parent joins Parents Without Partners or a similar group, you'll meet and spend time with others in discussion groups and family outings. Formally or informally, the points of view of single parents and their children will help you to look at your bereavement.

Suppose Your Parent Remarries

What if your surviving parent begins to date and eventually plans remarriage? Instead of being jubilant, you may be quite upset. Taking a stepparent (and possibly stepsiblings) into the household puts a major strain on you. And moving into theirs seems no better.

First, your family was whole. Then it was broken. And now there is the possibility that it will be repaired, remade, suddenly unbroken. Your parent, stepparent, and you probably all want to believe that it will turn out great, with harmony and love abounding. It's not at all surprising to find everyone involved utterly crushed, having found additional loneliness, emptiness, and loss instead of happiness.

Stepfamilies face ready-made problems. Stepparents do not have the legal rights of natural or adoptive parents. They have married their new spouses when those spouses were ready. The children, ready or not, have come along with the deal. Stepparents, while fond of their stepchildren, often may regard the care of these young people as a duty. What is more, the relationship stepparents have with their stepchildren is guaranteed only for as long as the marriage is. It's not the most secure of beginnings for either stepparents or stepchildren.

Neither stepparent nor stepchild knows the other very

well before the marriage, but both are burdened by the false idea that they will and must love one another. Some stepparents deeply want to help the youngsters they have come to live with, aiming to heal their past wounds. Yet, to the stepchild, the stepparent is often seen as a great threat.

How can love form instantly when someone new intrudes into the life you have set up with your surviving parent? Very likely there are special times you've grown to share. They're precious to you and have helped you to get through your loss. What's going to happen now?

Perhaps you've had responsibilities and acted as a substitute parent yourself. Now some "person" is on the scene, taking away some of your attention and duties. No wonder you fear you'll be losing instead of gaining.

But think of it from the stepparent's point of view for a moment.

The stepparent comes into a household where different values and habits have dominated for years. He or she likes concerts, hikes, and other excursions on Sundays; you like watching television or reading at home. Like you, the stepparent fears the loss of treasured activities.

The stepparent also must face one or more young people who compare him or her with the natural parent. Those youngsters tend to reach negative conclusions, sometimes without justification. And they're none too quiet about it, either. How would *you* like to hear a variation of "My father made better barbecues" several times a week?

Stepparents may even question if they were desired for themselves, or if they were acquired merely as housekeepers, breadwinners, or handy new parents. They sometimes have the problem of managing two groups of children in one household and treating them fairly and warmly so that neither natural children nor stepchildren could make charges of partiality or harshness. Not knowing if you need a firm hand or a fun parent, they may careen back and forth between the two. The inconsistency does not encourage healing of wounds.

Does all this sound easy? Not at all, and it's made even harder by the presence of the myth that perpetuates the idea that stepparents, particularly stepmothers, are calculating and mean, even witchlike. In *Snow White* and *Hansel and Gretel,* the stepmothers pretend they care for the children until after the marriage takes place and later reveal intentions to do away with them. And you've probably heard the saying, "She was treated like a stepchild."

In light of such stories and expressions, it comes as no surprise that many youngsters are apprehensive and embarrassed about having a stepparent. No one likes to be different, and our society fosters yet another falsehood: that normal families are nuclear, intact families. More than one adolescent has lied so that others will think a stepparent is a natural parent. But that same young person may be mortally wounded to see a new person being affectionate with the true parent. It somehow seems disloyal to the wonderful dead parent, and distresses the youngster no end.

Then there is another embarrassment, also involving loyalty to the lost one. How should your stepparent introduce you? What should you call this being who has entered your family? Mom or Dad is probably not right at the beginning. Alternatives are open to you, such as Papa Jack, Jack, Stepfather. They all involve being willing to communicate. Laura thought she had solved her nomenclature problem with her stepmother by refraining from using any name at all. One day, however, Laura was in the basement when the phone rang. The call was for her stepmother, who was three floors above, in the attic. Realizing her predicament, Laura dashed up the three flights of stairs to gasp breathlessly, "It's for you." Had the stepmother been granted a name, Laura could have saved steps and called from below.

In order to establish any semblance of harmony, honest communication is necessary. It's essential to admit that love doesn't grow overnight, and that each adult and child in this re-formed family has problems with the other. It's wise to acknowledge that the stepparent can never replace the natural parent, but that the family can attain some contentment if feelings are allowed to be spoken. If relaxed discussion can prevail, who knows? A bonus might be warmth without strain and, in time, even love.

The Death of a Sibling

For parents, the death of their child is one of the worst catastrophes that can possibly befall them. For the brothers and sisters of that child, it is also a devastating, shattering tragedy.

If your sibling died because of illness, the death may have been the climactic scene of a long, agonizing play in which the strength of the entire family was tested. During the illness, the parents have had to devote inordinate time, money, and energy to the sick child, often neglecting you. They may have tried to lie to you, hoping to protect you from bad news. This merely confused you and worried you because their faces revealed with certainty that something was desperately wrong.

You may have watched your brother or sister become sicker and sicker, standing by helplessly as rescue efforts did not work. In the book *The Magic Moth*, ten-year-old Maryanne is dying of heart disease. Her brother Mark-O is deeply unhappy yet relishes the daily opportunity to bring Maryanne something he has concocted especially for her. He looks forward to it while she lives and will remember it after she has died. If you had these moments to share with your sibling, perhaps you did not feel quite so powerless.

You read earlier about the guilt that is frequent when someone you love has died. Whether death is caused by illness, accident, or stillbirth, these feelings are intensified when the victim is a brother or sister. The thought that you were responsible lingers in the back of your mind. It's hard to get rid of it without a lot of talking.

You also read about fear. It's logical to be fearful after your brother or sister has died. "If one child in a family can die, why can't another?" you ask. You may have been so worried about it that you began to act sick. Perhaps illness seemed the only way to extricate your parents from their sorrow and get them to look at you.

The most helpful thing you can do if you're worried is to convince your parents to take you to a doctor, many times if necessary, so that you can begin to rest easy.

It's hard to return to normal after a brother or sister dies. It seems that nothing could shake up the family more. If the illness and death were not enough, it's an unfortunate fact that many outsiders are anything but helpful in the situation. Without doubt, some friends came forth and did what they could to support you in your crisis, but others surely made an abrupt and unexpected exit when they heard of the illness or accident. You and your parents were justified in feeling hurt and angry, but the reality is this: The death of a child overwhelms some people so much that they must withdraw.

Jeffrey Monaghan, a strapping college freshman, died after a freak football injury. His parents' good friends Bea and Jack couldn't bring themselves to go to the funeral or to pay a condolence call. "We just can't do it. Here we are with a healthy child. Elizabeth and Jeffrey played together from the time they were in carriages. How can we go see them? It's their only child; it's unspeakable." You can be sure that Bea and Jack have plenty of guilt, but it is indeed Bea and Jack who have the problem, not Jeffrey's parents. If something like this has happened to you, in time you may come to understand that peculiar behavior takes place because of something the other person lacks, not *you*. Then you may forgive them.

Harder to forgive are the culprits who, in ignorance or outright malice, do not withdraw, but instead create additional problems. Any adults who made fun of a terminally ill child or refused to allow their youngsters to be nearby because of the illness are culprits indeed. Any adults who, after your sibling's death, refused to allow their offspring to be with you are also culprits. They may merit forgiveness for one reason only: Their problem with death is so out of control that they have lost all of the compassion and logical thinking they ever possessed. They are in deep trouble.

Parents who lose a child sometimes fall into deep trouble as well. Like the outsiders, they may try to protect their remaining children beyond what is reasonable. Some won't let their youngsters play exuberantly, have a full social life, or take chances. Others try to undo the past by making surviving siblings perfect, insisting upon excellence in just about everything.

These reactions merely serve to make everyone miserable. A better route to regaining security is for parents and young people to seek help in discussion groups consisting of those who have undergone similar ordeals. Research and charity organizations have begun to sponsor groups, concentrating particularly on families who have lost children. In such settings, concerns for the future can be examined.

6

The Many Ways of Death

Was there ever a grief as painful as yours? When the end of bereavement is nowhere in sight, you may justifiably ask this question. Let no one deny your suffering, for no one has ever borne your particular sorrow. Shakespeare spoke to those who would deprecate or disparage one grief in favor of another when he wrote, "Everyone can master a grief but he that has it."

At the same time, however, the manner of some deaths present unique practical and psychological strain for survivors.

Accidental and Violent Deaths Are Shocking
Not everyone dies after a lengthy illness. Accidents and violent deaths, such as murder, are rare, but they cause many adults and children to die suddenly each year. One moment everything is fine and the next there is tragedy. Such deaths are more shocking. They increase the confusion and anger felt afterward and often intensify the guilt felt by parents and siblings. After seventeen-year-old Loren was killed in a car several miles from his

home, his parents doubted their wisdom in allowing him to go out with his friends the night of the accident. "We should have asked him to stay with Jessica. Baby-sitting would have kept him with us." This guilt does not make sense, of course, but it's hard to eradicate. Only after extended conversations with couples in similar crisis did Loren's parents begin to cope.

Murder, like a senseless accident, seems such a waste. It enrages survivors. And sometimes one person's anger turns into another's guilt. In frantic bewilderment, a family scapegoat may be selected before there is time for thought and consideration.

That's what happened in Myron's family. Myron's father ran a cleaning store. One summer evening, when Myron was twelve, his Dad descended the stairs from their apartment above the store, ready to resume business after dinner. "Go down and help Daddy," urged Myron's mother, as her son dawdled over dessert. Five minutes later a shot was heard. Myron's father was killed, the murderer never found. Myron's mother wailed, "If you had gone down, this never would have happened."

Myron has probably come to terms with his remorse; he's a father himself now. But he has taken some drastic steps to remove himself from the source of blame. Since he's been old enough to be on his own, he's made sure he lives at least 1,500 miles from his mother.

When death has taken place suddenly, it is wise to go more slowly in making decisions than after an expected illness. If guilt persists, counseling may be in order.

A Mysterious Killer

Great confusion and guilt also result when an infant dies of Sudden Infant Death Syndrome, also called crib death. In this syndrome, a baby, usually between the age of one week and seven months, is found dead in its crib. There is no apparent cause.

Right now, no one knows what causes SIDS or how to prevent it, but researchers are working on both. Doctors do know that it's not contagious, can't be inherited, and is not caused by vomiting or suffocation. They are working toward identifying infants who may be likely victims, hoping to monitor them closely with machinery in order to save them if respiratory difficulty arises.

Parents and siblings who must cope with SIDS feel so very guilty because the disease is not presently understood. Nor is it very widely known. Parents blame themselves for something *no one,* no matter how responsible, could have foreseen or prevented in terms of today's medical knowledge. Siblings blame themselves because, just when their jealousy was at its height, they seem to have succeeded in ridding the family of the crying, demanding new arrival. Perhaps when the death was first discovered, a distraught parent asked a surviving sibling, "Sam!!! What did you do?!" Later, when cause of death is understood, the accusation has already made its impact.

The families of SIDS infants are often maligned by the community. Because so few people have the facts on SIDS (and because the facts are few), neighbors and relatives pass remarks on the way the mother cared for herself during pregnancy or the possibility of "bad" genes in the family. Education of the public is one of the goals of the organizations concerned with SIDS; perhaps when more are knowledgeable, such insensitivity will diminish.

War Is Different
When someone dies in a war, the survivors feel the sorrow, denial, anger, and guilt experienced after other deaths. There is an important difference, though. When the death occurs, the intensity may not be as strong, its expression not as convulsive. If that occurs, it is because, to some extent, the survivors have long known of death's possibility and have rehearsed their reactions internally. Some of their feelings have already been expended in anticipatory mourning. But as one army mother said, "You're never really prepared, you always keep your hope." Upon the actual death, the survivors are already in a state of bereavement, but there is a great deal of mourning left to do.

Those involved in war deaths are not the only ones who go through some anticipatory grief. To a lesser extent, the families of police officers and firefighters live with constant underlying tension. They bear the burden of potential tragedy at all times. Hope predominates, but realism dictates awareness.

Terminal Illness
The families of terminally ill patients are another group who go through anticipatory grief. For them, there

may be very little hope, therefore many physical symptoms befall them before their relative dies. With the end in sight, survivors-to-be also react with the denial, bargaining ("If I am kind forever after, God, will you please let her live?"), and rage associated with bereavement. By the time of death, the survivors often have reached the point of acceptance. People who die slowly because of illness share a unique position in life. In their terminal sickness, they have both the burden and opportunity to contemplate the end of their own existence. They do so with greater urgency and sharpness than the rest of the population.

Most medical practitioners of this generation believe that the dying should be openly told of their conditions. At the same time, there should always be room for realistic hopes of recovery. There are instances of remission and cure.

With today's mass media exposure of cancer, muscular dystrophy, and other life-shortening illnesses, most victims, whether told or not, are fully aware of their chances for survival. If the information is not shared, those who are dying, young or old, are left to suffer the lonely isolation of carrying on a charade with family, friends, and medical staff. The thoughts of everyone concerned are about dying, but expression of feeling is closed off. It is impossible to maximize whatever time is left, to finish up life's business, and to say good-bye to loved ones.

For some people, knowledge of impending death heralds great personal growth. To be kept in the dark denies them their dignity, inhibiting any progression they might make toward coming to terms with what fate has dealt. As such, it robs them of any peace they might have. To quote noted thanatologist Robert Kavanaugh, "Knowledge is kindness, ignorance is cruel." What is more, the atmosphere of secrecy forebodes ill for survivors' expression of grief.

Until recently, researchers paid little attention to the responses of the dying. The formal study of thanatology (grief and loss) has burst upon the scene as a major subscience only in the past ten years. Until then, many scientists thought it was improper to investigate feelings at such a time. Others merely gave up on the dying, regarding them as already dead. Today, the idea of death as an obscenity is fading.

Thanatologists can now offer information of great help to families trying to understand a world they cannot enter—the world of those who are about to die.

Dr. Elisabeth Kübler-Ross is probably most famous of all thanatologists. A psychiatrist who has counseled hundreds of terminally ill patients, she speaks of five stages the dying may go through.

The first stage is called Shock and Denial. In many loss experiences, an initial response is to try to undo the situation. "No, not me," is said at this time. A certain amount of denial is good, for it allows people to concentrate on daily life without paralyzing fear. However, people whose state of illness implies they will probably die within a year are demonstrating greater denial than is healthy if they make plans for a trip three years hence.

During the second stage, called Anger, dying people recognize what is happening to them and hate it. The question becomes "Why me?" As they ask why their lives have taken this downward turn, they may become difficult to be with, stormy, and bitter. Someone is needed to listen to their complaints and to continue listening without falsely trying to cheer them up.

The third stage is Bargaining. If they have to die, the patients ask favors before they depart. They are saying, "Yes, me, but . . ." They may turn especially kind, hoping their good behavior will allow them to live until a special date, such as a birthday, family wedding, graduation, or other event.

And the fourth stage is Depression. Fully acknowledging their illness ("Yes, me."), they realize they will soon lose everything and everyone they have ever loved. Moreover, they themselves will be lost. Their sadness overwhelms them, and they, too, need a patient ear. As depression continues, dying patients begin preparing for death, grieving in anticipation. As unfinished business becomes completed, visitors may no longer be welcomed. Instead of being a symptom of anger, it is a signal of growing quiet.

The final stage is Acceptance. Patients are reconciled with the coming event. While they are not happy, they are saying, "My time is very close now and it's all right." If there has been great pain, they may welcome death.

Dr. Kübler-Ross stresses that not everyone reaches the final emotional reactions. She advises that patients jump back and forth among the stages, perhaps being involved in two or more simultaneously. In addition, the dying may not approach the stages in traditional order.

Another thanatologist, Dr. Stephen Gullo, has looked at dying patients another way, categorizing six styles of coping. Like Kübler-Ross, he feels people die in the manner that makes them most comfortable and that they may utilize more than one approach. Unlike Kübler-Ross, though, Gullo doesn't speak of stages to be passed through but refers instead to patterns. "We die as we have lived," he says.

One style of coping is the Death Acceptor. These people struggle to live with progressing illness but realistically assess their chances without lying to themselves. When resources have been exhausted and things look dim, they grieve for their losses.

In opposition are the Death Deniers. Most acknowledge a state of illness but refuse to accept its gravity. Or they might insist they will be the miraculous ones to beat the rap. Gullo points out that in order to continue, denial is a game that cannot be played alone.

Death Submitters employ another approach. They cannot accept, and they cannot deny, they can only give in, totally overwhelmed by their helplessness. Believing their efforts will be to no avail, they often discard medicine or reject valid good news as lies. They see themselves as doomed, passive victims unable to wage battle against fate.

Death Facilitators are in another category. They more actively seek to aid in their own deaths. It is hard to sway them from their refusal of medication. In the extreme, they may commit suicide. It is not that they wish to die. On the contrary, they wish to live, but they cannot go on living with the ravages of terminal illness.

Another coping style is that of the Death Transcender. To these individuals, death is one part of a larger outlook on life. They may accept it as the precursor to afterlife, intertwined with religious importance. Or they may simply view death as life's final stage. Death transcenders are rarely children.

The final coping style is Death Defiance, characterized by ceaseless battle with fate. While they do accept the eventual outcome, for as long as possible they will hang on, enjoying whatever they can and maintaining their independence. While Death Submitters might become dependent upon wheelchairs before it is truly necessary, Death Defiers refuse to be confined, even if their struggle exhausts them.

When you are aware of some of the feelings dying people have, it may become easier to talk with someone who is dying. The work of Kübler-Ross and others indicates that the dying appreciate a chance to discuss their illnesses. What is really needed, after all, is someone who is willing to talk and listen—both to everyday concerns and to thoughts about dying. A group of Alaskan Indians accomplish this quite naturally. When someone is close to death, a priest is called in. The dying person makes plans for survivors' adjustments, tells stories of their lives together, and prays for all. This constitutes a farewell.

It is ideal if at least one member of a dying person's family is able to listen to that person's deepest concerns and wishes. Unfortunately, families are not always willing. Hospital staffs and counseling agencies in some areas have begun to fill the need. They utilize the counseling skills of individuals who, with or without professional training, are up to handling the formidable task of listening, staying nearby, and listening some more. If someone in your family needs more opportunities for talk than are available at home, a thanatological counselor might be sought out.

When Death Is Self-Inflicted

More people die at their own hands than is commonly realized. Motivated by great unhappiness, twice as many people kill themselves as kill others, making suicide the tenth leading cause of death in our society. However, statistics on the frequency of suicide by young people vary: some studies rank it fourth, others, second in frequency.

The figures are even more alarming because the actual rate of self-inflicted death is believed to be much greater than the statistics above indicate. Families and physicians cover up suicides, because of stigma. Some religious groups take the position that God will judge, while others consider suicide a sin against God. Finally, suicide is hidden because it is often regarded as a major flaw in the family structure. In addition to the many suicides never reported as such, attempts at self-destruction outnumber successful suicides by the fantastic ratio of 100:1.

What tempts people into taking their own lives?

Mental pain is the underlying cause, but there seem to be two different categories of death by suicide. One takes place when an individual seeks to escape what seems to be an intolerable situation. For an adult this might happen after a dreadfully long period of unemployment or when a gigantic scandal threatens to "ruin life." For a young person, the draw toward extinction might be caused by unwarranted academic pressure, being threatened by a gang, or being plagued by excessive guilt. In all these examples, the people think—perhaps mistakenly—there is no workable solution to their problems.

The second type of suicide has been called instrumental. In dying, the people wish magically to influence someone else. Be they adults or youngsters, they are trying to say, "Do something." During the Vietnam war, two American teenagers created and carried through a peace pact in which they hoped their suicides would be seen as courageous protest statements. Eliot Asinof wrote about it in *Craig and Joan: Two Lives for Peace*.

Instrumental suicides take place for self-centered and less lofty causes as well. In actuality, though, this group often does not seek death, but searches for new hope instead. The hope would come from a help-giving reaction from those surrounding them. Unfortunately, however, if they leave no escape mechanism for rescue, no one can listen to what they had to say.

With either type of suicide or attempt, a look back in time usually shows that the victims had given signals of heading in that direction for some time. Rarely are there sudden suicides without traceable symptoms and causes.

Families often minimize the distress flags of suicide attempts as showing off. This can be a disastrous mistake. Instead of dismissing self-destructive behavior as manipulative, deep concern should be shown. Early tip-offs of (potential) suicide include extended and deep despair, acute withdrawal, or severe proneness to accident.

Most people who attempt suicide are later found to have been deeply depressed for an excessive period. Depression doesn't always show itself as gloom; it can be masked, appearing in such forms as apathy, hypochondria, drug-taking, or sexual promiscuity. Whatever its form, a low, low feeling underlies all outward expressions. Many suicidal individuals feel inferior to others. Many feel unloved, and many say they are extremely lonely.

In some young people, suicide can be an attempt to punish parents—one which may be prompted by a small disagreement. In other youngsters, it is used as a means to run from blame and guilt. In still others, suicide is seen as a way to rejoin a loved one who has died.

Some people are especially prone to self-destructive behavior. Among these are the teenagers and adults who have endured more than their share of illness—victims of kidney disease, leukemia, and other conditions. Because of continuing ill health, it is understandable that they fall prey to depression. For that reason and others, the chronically and terminally ill can benefit greatly from expert counseling by a hospital staff to help them cope.

What about the survivors?

Being the survivor of any death is difficult. Suicide

doubles the difficulty and multiplies the complications. As said earlier, because of the stigma, suicide is often kept secret. The act becomes sticky material for webs of conspiracy with which survivors defend themselves against the critical eyes of the outside world.

If you are a survivor, it's possible you are under pressure to keep a secret that probably can't be kept. You probably also endure the added element of rejection. Sadly and undeniably, this person made a conscious choice to leave the world as we know it. Whatever caused the suicide, the feeling of rejection is genuine and cannot be dismissed as imaginary. It must be worked through.

If you are the survivor of a family suicide, your guilt is probably deep. Even though you've been told time and again that it's untrue, you may not be able to erase from your mind the possibility that your insolent behavior or ill-wishes precipitated the act.

You may feel you failed. If you were instructed to watch the person but didn't prevent the suicide, your guilt is great. Because self-destructive patterns show themselves well in advance of the act, placing such responsibility upon your shoulders was unfair. Nonetheless, your self-blame continues.

You feel especially guilty if you were in the unfortunate position of being aware that your loved one was preparing for death. Perhaps you watched helplessly as a desperate family member brought a gun into the house. Maybe you knew someone was harboring a large number of sleeping pills without a prescription. If you told no one, you may feel you acted as an assistant. Even if you recognized signs, it isn't your fault.

Sometimes the survivors of suicide go to an extreme in order to avoid "catching death." Adam did this. His father had jumped from a ten-story building to end his insoluble alcoholism. Adam was fifteen then; he vowed never to take a drink. He is now a man of forty and has kept his vow. That may be a healthy response, and one that does not affect life much. But that's not all Adam won't do. He also refuses to be in high places. His inability to enter a tall office building or fly in a plane is not so healthy. It has affected his life and career decisions.

Adam fights suicide in the only ways he knows, but he is still in trouble. Other survivors are attracted to it as a way out of problems. In many families, there is a tradition of suicide; survivors in such instances are often resigned to it, expecting eventually to succumb to its temptation.

Suicide is brutal. The problems of surviving suicide are unique, complex, and very difficult. Professional counseling is highly recommended if you are that survivor. Talking out your reactions and fears with a highly trained person is crucial to maintaining mental health and hope after a family suicide.

7

Living with the Survivors

When someone in a family has died, the entire group is devastated. It is as though the fabric of the family were ripping apart right at the center. This is true no matter which person in the family has died, adult or child. For a time, each survivor feels, like Humpty Dumpty, that there has been a great fall. Each must try, with help such as Humpty Dumpty had or alone, to put himself or herself back together again, so that the family fabric can remain durable. Unlike eggs, human spirits can be repaired, damages bandaged.

During the course of trying to become whole again, it is helpful to have information about problems that may pop up.

Families Will Fight

For as long as there will be families, there will continue to be family disagreements. One might expect that the sobering nature of death would put an end to squabbles, but it doesn't always work that way. With emotion at its peak, grief may be transferred onto small issues, thereby reflected away from self.

Families have been known to fight before a funeral over how it will be conducted. Who will officiate? When and where should it be held? Who will sit where? Who will pay for what? The list of possibilities is endless, and resentment can continue afterward as well: Why did so-and-so wear that inappropriate outfit? Why didn't this one or that one show up? Some questions, such as the last, are evidence of genuine hurt, while others are displacement for wrenching pain.

And on it goes. In some families division of property is cause for animosity, bringing out resentments that have lain dormant for years. In some families, one member might accuse another of mistreating the dead relative years earlier, perhaps projecting their own guilt for misunderstandings that remained without reconciliation.

In many homes, it is mourning itself that is a target for bitterness. One relative may claim another has come out of bereavement too soon. Or the unhappiness may be over members who, others feel, mourn either too long or too loud. Finally, in some families, excuses are not needed. Unaccountable rage merely takes over in times of bereavement.

In all these cases, it is best to communicate openly. Without confusing accusation with tactful attempt to weed out problems, it might be good during calm discussion to bear in mind some underlying questions. These can be asked of yourself and others:

Why is each person *really* feeling this way?

What is actually being said when each person acts this way?

Is the problem real?

Is it worthy of the amount of attention it is getting?

If the problem is not real, is it a cover-up for unexpressed grief?

How might that grief be expressed in another way?

Is the help of outsiders needed in order to get mourning back on the track?

Angels Never Walk the Earth

In many families, after a member dies, the survivors create a halo around that person. Every accomplishment becomes marvelous; every negative trait is kept hidden beneath the surface, unspoken.

Encouraging only good talk and thoughts about the dead may be harmful. First, it makes that person's life more wondrous than it actually was; you take longer to bring yourself to accept the death. Second, if you never come to see the person as a human being with failings, you can get stuck with a different type of problem. As the survivor, you can never hope to be as remarkable. Having created an angel, your earthlike behavior will never match up. You then feel twice as guilty for your own survival. If it goes far enough, you may even wish to trade one of the survivors (perhaps yourself) for the return of the fallen angel.

It's better to talk openly about the bad times along with the good. If Dad took you many places but also teased you mercilessly when you got there, it's healthier to remember both parts of the picture. If your sister was very smart, but also used her intelligence to trick you out of your share, it's best to talk about the double-edged nature of her sword. If you go over both the good and the bad, you can come to terms with the person as he or she really was. In time, the meaning of your loved one's life will have perspective.

Overprotection

Once a family has lost someone, it is most natural that some of the survivors should worry an extra bit about other survivors. Unfortunately, it can turn into a big, complicated headache if *you* are the one being treated as a piece of porcelain. Patricia Olson was in that predicament. After her father died in an accident, her mother kept an eagle eye out for her eleven-year-old daughter. Every move Patricia made was evaluated in terms of its safety. Pat, too, feared losing anyone further in her life, and so happily fell into her mother's possessiveness. Before long, the two of them were staying in together a great deal. Pat quickly forgot how to travel to music lessons, complete her homework herself, even how to make a bed—all chores most eleven-year-olds have mastered. Pat's mother convinced herself that she should help her daughter with these and other tasks. "The poor girl has no father," she said. "I must make it up to her."

Although Pat had more than the normal amount of help from her mother, she didn't fail to catch her mother's message and take full advantage. As the pitied half-orphan, she demanded more and more things: clothing, jewelry, records. If denied, she subtly played upon her mother's heartstrings as the product of a broken home.

The games these two were playing prevented each from growing. Pat's classmates had begun excluding her and privately called her "Precious Pat." Pat's mother was so busy being chauffeur and nursemaid that she closed herself off from meeting men and women with whom she had something in common.

Pat is nineteen now. The games could have continued to this day and into Pat's adult years if Pat's Aunt Lynn had not noticed the change in their behavior and sat them both down for several long talks. A lot of tears and emotions were shed. Pat still seems young and withdrawn in comparison to those her own age. But those discussions started both mother and daughter back on their feet.

Patricia's Aunt Lynn had wisdom because of her own experience as a child. At the age of ten, Lynn's older brother had died of rheumatic fever while Lynn was at school. In her mind, Lynn decided that future attendance at school might result in further deaths. She developed stomachaches and refused to go. How lacking her parents were of compassion, she thought, when they bundled her off to school, even dragged her there some mornings, as she kicked and screamed. Later Lynn realized that her parents were right to put a stop to her school phobia. They knew that if they let her indulge her fears, they would be confirming their reality, when in fact they were unfounded. No one would disappear if

Lynn separated from her family each day. Lynn spoke with Patricia and her mother about overprotection and helped them see the direction in which they were heading.

Expecting Too Much

The opposite of protecting too much is failing to protect enough. Some families fall into the habit of treating their survivors as replacements for the dead person, placing heavy burdens upon their shoulders.

Have you known a family like the Rockwells? Just a few years ago, they were five healthy people. Then Mamie Rockwell, the mother, developed a degenerative nerve disease that would eventually kill her. By the time she died last spring, a gradual change had already taken place. The oldest girl, Becky, had slowly been transformed into a mother-wife substitute. At fifteen, she is already exhausted from trying to balance an academic program with meeting the needs of her father and younger siblings. Becky shops, cooks, and cleans without assistance or words of thank-you. Her blue eyes look glazed, her face older than those of her classmates in sophomore year. In spite of her resentment and fatigue, Becky will say she *should* be doing all these chores.

On rare occasions, a youngster who has taken over a parent's role will be urged to spend the night in the bed of the surviving parent. Little and not-so-little boys may be asked to comfort their lonely mothers, and small and older girls may be asked to help their fathers feel better. Despairing parents may press for sexual contact with their children. It is sad that an adult is lonely; you may feel very sorry for your mother or father and want to give physical solace. Sharing a bed is not a good solution for the problem of loneliness. Young people belong in their own beds, as do all parents. If you are having trouble with a parent who insists, talk to another adult about the problem immediately.

Cluster Families Are a Help

Whether your problem is overprotection, underprotection, or some other difficulty, you and your fellow survivors may find the idea of a cluster family appealing. A cluster family is a group of families who band together for various reasons that usually involve loss. Some have moved and live too far from relatives to see them frequently. Others are single-parent families because of divorce or death. There are many other possible reasons, as you can well imagine.

Cluster families are together because of changes in modern living, which have led to loneliness. In past generations, people lived among extended families. That meant relatives of several generations lived either in the same house or within a short distance of one another. There was usually someone to rely upon if one member were sick or otherwise needed attention. In an extended family, it was reassuring that someone could always be counted on to give advice and keep the family running smoothly.

Today, about twenty percent of us move each year. It's

not rare to have one's relatives living two or three thousand miles away. Far from their roots, small nuclear families live in homes with only two generations present—parents and their children. They wonder: Who can we turn to with everyday problems? Who will help us in an emergency?

The cluster family tries to accomplish what the extended family did. It works this way: Several families get together. Sometimes it is under the direction of a local church, synagogue, Parents Without Partners chapter, or other community agency; sometimes it is initiated by the individuals. They grow to know one another better by formally scheduling events, such as picnics, trips to the movies, and book discussion sessions. Some of the events are planned for families, others for adults only.

Before long, the cluster family becomes more than much-needed company for one another. After a time, if the group goes well, they have committed themselves to listening, being there, and helping in crises. The cluster family can be a source of knowledge and aid in intimate matters, possibly including financial and medical considerations. The cluster family can serve an additional function. Just as might happen within the extended family, a young person who has lost a relative or friend could form a new attachment with another member of the cluster family. That person could, in part, substitute for the lost individual. Often, it is when a substitute relationship comes on the scene that the bereaved person first allows mourning to be expressed. The presence of the new person may enable the mourner to work toward restructuring life. A cluster family doesn't promise this but offers a place where it might happen.

The Strain of Mourning

When any family has suffered a loss, its members are under great stress. Studies in the United States and Great Britain indicate that adult survivors sometimes suffer a rise in frequency of disease following significant loss. One of the researchers, Dr. Murray Parkes, implies that if heart disease develops, it is because people under emotional strain tend to increase their ingestion of deleterious products, including starches, fats, nicotine, and caffeine. Other research shows that survivors whose family members died of terminal disease may later turn up ill because they were forced to ignore already existing conditions while caring for their loved ones. Another investigator, Dr. Melvin Krant, feels that physical or mental deterioration is likely only if mourning work is not carried out satisfactorily.

Major loss is often accompanied by additional losses. For example, the death of an adult family member is likely to lead to a change in financial status. There could be less income. And the death of any family member will probably lead to alterations in social activity. Some friends may overextend themselves to you in your bereavement when they really can no longer be sociable at all. "Come for a weekend," they might say, but a date is never set. Their philosophies will not allow them to be reminded of death. You are disappointed but must accept their limitations.

These changes constitute loss, as do any altered circumstances in daily life, including some that might appear to be happy events. Vacationing means you lose sleeping in your own bed. Marrying means you may lose familiar surroundings and the company of those with whom you grew up.

Recognizing that death is but one loss experience, Dr. Thomas Holmes has compiled a list of life events that involve stress. Feeling that there is a relationship between a person's total number of life changes in any year and resulting medical problems, Holmes devised a scale whereby the impact of particular events is measured. Death of a close family member is allotted 63 units; marriage, 50; and change in schools, 20. An account of alteration in circumstances can be kept. If 200 or more "life-change" points are accumulated in a given year, it is possible that the person is being pushed beyond endurance. That may lead to physical or mental breakdown. The scale, included in the Appendix, can be used to become aware of periods when changes should be avoided. During the year following the shocking event, it is a fact that your chances of becoming ill are greater.

There are several additional things you can do to keep your chances of becoming ill as slim as possible.

First, go to a doctor for a checkup. Advise other survivors to go, too. If you're well, the examination will relieve any fears you have of contracting the illness that may have killed your relative or friend. If symptoms you show are not normal signs of bereavement, a skilled physician will pick this up and keep your condition from deteriorating. During the first year after the death, see the doctor as often as you think necessary. If it reassures you, it's worth the trouble and expense.

Keep yourself fit by resting adequately. Your body is in the process of repairing itself. It may need more sleep, and it certainly needs a well-balanced diet high in protein. Give it what it asks for.

To mourn well, you need energy. Set up your days so that your emotions are able to find respite, along with your body. This is not the time to be running helter-skelter after school, careening from hockey to piano lessons to scouts and back to ceramics. Neither is it the time for older survivors to participate in a dizzying cycle of weekly commitments.

Advisors to the bereaved often mistakenly urge them to keep busy, to develop interests. While this may serve as temporary reprieve from pain, if too many hobbies are developed, the mourner will be spending all available resources on pursuits other than mourning. The survivor will be running away, yet will fail to escape the state of bereavement. It's unproductive to bathe in self-pity, but it's also unproductive to stay so busy that none of one's strength remains to do the important task of mourning.

Besides clearing time, you can make yourself available for mourning in several additional ways.

If you keep your body and mind relatively free of medication, you can better experience your pain. Turning to the corner peddler for uppers, downers, and other addictive measures will take you away from the act of mourning. But it will not make it disappear. While you may be upset, to start a cigarette habit now will not benefit your health. Being part of the smoking crowd will not fill your emptiness, either. As much as possible, leave yourself open for good, painful, exhausting mourning.

Should you decide to be addiction-free, an odd complication might make it harder for you. Often adult survivors may urge samples of their own sedatives upon you. Before the funeral, someone may hand you a tranquilizer. On an anniversary of the death, the story may be the same. Human beings sometimes overlook opportunities to rely upon their own capacities for resilience and understanding. Because they fear meeting pain head-on, they may fail to recognize potential strength, which is considerable. Remind them.

The height of bereavement is a time to keep decision-making to a minimum. How tempting it is to pick up roots and start over somewhere new! However, many people who, right after a death in the family, choose to move, start new jobs, change schools, or dispose of large amounts of property, come to regret it. The mind is in turmoil, ill-prepared for wisdom and forethought.

Urge adult survivors to hold off on major changes, especially those involving money. While matters may be pressing, they usually can wait until minds are clear. More than a week can be taken to dispose of property. Larger decisions such as trading a city apartment for suburban living should be weighed for months. Undertaken in the mistaken idea that changes will diminish the loss already suffered, hasty solutions can create additional problems and additional feelings of loss. You and other survivors should be wary of complicating your bereavement without need if you don't have to.

One final word on living with the survivors. Live with them. Take your time for solitude but don't confuse it with isolation. Keep surrounding yourself with life—plants, animals, and humans. The task of mourning is to be able to invest once again in human relationships after one such relationship has been severed. By keeping growing things around you, your return to wholeness is likely to be more rapid.

8

The Legacy of Survivors

When someone close to you dies, it's natural to feel deserted and alone for a while, wondering if you are less substantial than before. In time, grief will fade; bereavement will end as you mourn. But for now, think about it. You are not alone. Your importance is not diminished, for the person has left so much that you can carry with you always.

First, you have probably been left some things you can touch or look at. As part of the dead person's will, you may have been left some money to use later. Money is far from the most important thing you have been given, but in the eyes of the deceased, you were deemed special. Some families set aside money left in wills, spending it not on groceries, but on something that can be pointed to as a significant gift from someone they loved. If it is a large sum, the inheritance might buy a college education or a new car.

Even with smaller sums, the dead person can be remembered. When the author's grandfather died and left her two hundred dollars, she invited her family to join her in a weekend at a hotel, dubbing it "The Harry Weckstein Memorial Weekend." The old gentleman would have laughed heartily; the merriment in his name will be treasured.

Besides money, you may also inherit property—possibly furniture, apparel, household goods, hobby equipment, or handicrafts. If you have been given these or other objects, they, too, are treasures, for seeing and using them can momentarily bring you closer to the memories you have of the dead person. Some of this property will probably become very meaningful to you. One day, while you and your children examine your lives, asking where you are headed, you may use the inherited property to show your children proof of where your family and friends have been and what their interests were.

The objects of art and utility that your ancestors created or acquired are very real reminders of the continuity of life. The influence these artifacts played in shaping your generation may be reflected upon and appreciated.

When we die, we can leave more than possessions. We can leave part or all of our bodies if we arrange it before death. Today, kidneys, corneas, and hearts are taken from the dead so that others may live in health. Whole bodies become cadavers needed desperately at medical schools, ensuring that tomorrow's doctors can adequately study the human body. Usually, the close friends and relatives of the dead are not the direct recipients of the organ transplants, nor do they themselves investigate the cadaver. The survivors benefit greatly anyway, knowing their loved one has given, even in the end. They feel good inside because someone they were close to helped further medical progress and diminish human suffering.

Property, possessions, money, organs, these are all tangible gifts that may have been left you. But there is more given to you that cannot be held in hand, which is of much greater importance.

If the person who died was a relative, some of the same genetic makeup was passed on to you. Ray Bradbury has spoken about the value of hereditary continuity. He tells of his father.

> He's been dead sixteen years and there isn't a day I haven't missed him. But the great thing is, you look at the backs of your hands and the knuckles and the hairs and he's THERE! He's in the cells, he's in the blood. I sense a proximity here of his flesh and mine that's fantastic . . . It's a great comfort. That's where immortality is—in the blood.

You, too, have a lineal heritage to think about and enjoy. The genetic heritage is transmitted at time of conception and will be passed on to future generations. But heredity is only one form of legacy. At birth, each of us also becomes subject to many other types of heritage that are passed on and left to us.

One form of this heritage is tradition. Every family has traditions. These need not stop at death but can be left to the next generation to continue. Every summer Ira Robbins and his family spend a month at Cape Cod. It's been that way for as long as Ira can remember; his father recalls nothing different, as this is a tradition *he* inherited from *his* parents, who have been dead for many years.

Your family may feel it cannot maintain its traditions because the very person who died was relied upon for carrying out the ritual. Traditions needn't come to a halt, though. They can go on in an altered form. Members of two families can get together to continue some of the good times.

One example of such effort takes place in Doris Buchanan Smith's book, *A Taste of Blackberries*. Jamie and his good friend frequently gather blackberries, which they give to their mothers. After Jamie dies tragically from a rare allergy to insect bites, his friend thoughtfully takes over for him in a small way. It is he who brings Jamie's mother berries.

Another example is seen in Meg Roemer's family every Thanksgiving. Since the death of Meg's father, her mother hasn't had the energy or desire to fuss over Thanksgiving dinner. Yet she wants to be with her children on this family holiday. To solve the problem, she and another widowed friend meet with both their children at a special neighborhood restaurant. There, for many different reasons, families come to celebrate amidst noise and good fellowship. It's a compromise, that's true, and doesn't compare with the old days when Meg's father was there, but as Meg and her mother say, "This is a blend of traditions old and new."

Along with the traditions of your family, you have been

left their values and personality qualities. You are likely to view human behavior and aspirations in much the same way as your relatives, largely because you've spent so much time with them. No doubt you've heard the saying, "The apple doesn't fall far from the tree." This means that you are likely to enlarge upon some of the patterns set by your ancestors. Such patterns don't stop upon death or separation.

If most of your relatives and their friends have gone to college or sought intellectual growth, it is probable that you, too, will travel that route. Even if a parent's death makes it financially difficult to get an education, the drive will probably have been planted in you by your early surroundings. You might have to fight harder to get it, but you are likely to try.

What Will You Remember?

The traditions and values given you are part of a larger legacy. That is the legacy of memories. There is a saying in the Talmud which instructs, "The righteous need no memorials, their words and deeds are their remembrances." It's true. By talking and thinking about the personal qualities of the person you loved and by reviving the moments in time you shared, memories remain animated as a continuing part of your life. So long as you do not hold out hope for the individual's return and are ready to meet new people and adventures, the memories—good and bad—can be a treasure of mind.

Your memories will be as individual as you are.

Andy Wood remembers his Uncle Eddie. At family

parties, he could be relied upon to entertain all the children. They clamored for his attention, vied for his knee. Uncle Eddie knew more limericks than anyone; his jokes and riddles were just the corny kind little ones enjoy. "What did the big rose say to the little rose?" he would ask. "Hiya, Bud!!!!" the children would scream. Tirelessly, Eddie would be available throughout the evening.

That was over ten years ago. Andy knows now that his uncle was not all fun and games. Some special kind of misery was there, too, an unhappiness that led to his suicide several years ago. Andy doesn't know for sure but imagines now that the amount of time Uncle Eddie spent with children said something about how deeply uncomfortable he was with adults.

Leah Morris remembers her neighbor Alfred. He had been retired for many years, and took great pleasure in tending a small garden and going for long walks. An amateur geographer at heart, Alfred would draw small maps for his jaunts. At times he'd devise a new shortcut to get somewhere; other times he'd purposely stretch out a trip to take as long as possible. Whenever Leah was home from fifth grade, Alfred would let her come along. The map was always a fascinating surprise. And while walking, Alfred showed Leah the beauty of city life. Before her walks with Alfred, Leah didn't know that fire hydrants came in several shapes and sizes; she didn't know that sewer design was an art form. Leah could make a long list: Alfred had taught her so much.

Alfred lived to be ninety-one. By the end, he was senile. Leah, a high school student, would occasionally go to visit him, but he didn't remember her. It hurt Leah when Alfred would confuse her with several other girls, even with local boys. But, in thinking back, Leah is grateful for the good years, for it was Alfred who gave Leah a keen eye.

One fall afternoon, Kevin's cat Buffy went under the house to die. Now, three years later, as Kevin drifts off to sleep, he often thinks about Buffy—how he would curl up in Kevin's bed, how he'd be scolded for ripping upholstery, how he loved to play with old newspapers, and how Kevin hated to clean Buffy's smelly litter box. Kevin is busy with cross-country skiing and marathon bicycling this year. He doesn't have need for another pet right now, but he hasn't forgotten that Buffy died. He also remembers that Buffy lived.

What Have You Been Left?

Look yourself over carefully. Yes, your world has been turned upside down. Someone close to you has died. But feeling alone and deserted is only part of the story.

What is your legacy?

Have you been left money to use in a memorable way? Have you been left property to cherish?

Do you share the same genes? Which body features do you have that the dead person also had?

In what ways was your loved one unique? How did they influence you?

What memories do you treasure about the dead person? Did you share a day so wonderful you'd wished it would go on forever? Was there ever a day spent together you'd wished had never happened? What were the times in-between like?

These things—property, genes, outlook, values, traditions, personal qualities, memories, and more—have been given to you. You are not any less because you have gone through a death experience. You have been left a rich legacy.

⑨

Some Final Words

"Trouble is Opportunity in Workclothes"

Mourning is painful; there's no doubt about it. But it can enable you to grow because each loss teaches.

Mourning teaches patience. Were you to stand on your head for a week, you couldn't bring back the person you loved. As there's nothing you can do, you're forced to learn that all wishes cannot be gratified. That's a lesson many of your friends probably do not yet fully appreciate.

Mourning teaches perspective. Those who've never had a catastrophe often overreact to small incidents, such as losing a few dollars, and are unable to cope when they are confronted with real obstacles. You are in a position that often enables you to distinguish the trivial worry from the significant consequence. Perhaps you've noticed that you now respond more appropriately and with greater calmness than you showed earlier.

Mourning teaches about depth and range of feeling. Before your bereavement, you probably never imagined the human soul was capable of so many fears, resentments, and kinds of sadness. You never imagined you loved so deeply. If you mourn, you acknowledge all these deep feelings and give yourself over to them. In an earlier chapter, the dead person was said to be in a room with a closed door. To be able to open the door and allow the sadness, anger, and other emotions to flow reflects maturity.

The mourning that you do helps you to see yourself and others more clearly. It can help you to understand why people sometimes act as they do. If your grandmother flares up and screams seemingly without provocation, you begin to have ideas about why such things occur. If your friend shrinks from view for a while when his father remarries, you may know what caused the disappearing act.

Because mourning offers understanding, it also helps you to treasure other survivors. At times, it is death that turns family rancor into reconciliation. The company of your family and friends, especially if times are difficult, takes on new importance. With each day more precious, you may remember to let others know what they mean to you. Trying to seize the moment fully, you appreciate the beauty in routine surroundings.

So much seems different now. In an odd way, changes can be an added plus. Because of your bereavement, you've probably gotten to know some interesting people, people who think in ways new to you. Is it being a Pollyanna to say that bereavement may have added a dimension to your existence?

Bereavement can be a period in which you achieve greater responsibility. Because of the changed circumstances in your home, you may hold an after-school job for the first time. Or you may be forced to learn to cook, sew, or install light bulbs. You may learn to take care of younger children or watch over sums of money.

In some families, bereavement does not imply new chores or encumbrances. Yet mourning may impel you, entirely on your own, to try something novel. Simply to forget, you might seek a job. Or you might let out your sadness through a medium you had never used to express anything else, such as poetry, painting, or music. Perhaps you are like Marie de France. During the Middle Ages, she said, "To put away my grief, I purposed to commence a booke."

Whether new tasks are thrust upon you or it is you who have chosen to give them a whirl, when you do new things well, you gain a happiness about your capabilities that helps you grow.

And you're growing in other very important ways, too. Because of your mourning, you know a great deal about who you are. You have reason to examine your identity and heritage in ways those who haven't been bereaved may not. You can begin to answer the questions, "Who am I?", "Where do I come from?", and "Where am I heading?"

Your experience with death has taught you that life will not stretch on without end. Most young people don't deny this, but they don't feel it in their bones; they imagine life offers an unlimited span for the fulfillment of dreams.

Life is finite. You know that the length of a life is but one measure; its quality is equally important. You know, too, that it's not too early to begin to construct goals for your body and mind. You're well aware that the way you live now will help determine both how long and how well you will survive.

Following a death, it is easier to see that it can be faced better if the challenge to live fully also has been met. Bereavement may be one of the things that helps you toward a stay on earth reminiscent of John Mills's poem: "Life's race well run, / Life's work well done, / Life's victory won, / Now cometh rest."

Every so often, it's helpful to ask yourself what you would do if you only had one year to live. The responses you give define your concept of a full, meaningful life. If you ask the question now and then, you are likely to act upon some of your thoughts, even though you are well. It's a way to recognize your real goals and priorities and make plans to pursue some of them.

Without doubt, bereavement is an opportunity to come to know yourself and to mature. You're still here, managing your bereavement, going on with your life, and growing. Death and loss are terrible, but being part of them did show that you could confront and overcome difficulties. Now you feel a special pride, strength, and courage to meet each day, because you have earned your own respect.

Further Reading

Books about Death: Nonfiction

Bernstein, Joanne E., and Gullo, Stephen. *When People Die.* New York: Dutton, 1976. (Ages 5–9)
  The death of one woman brings about questions of living, dying, and losing.

Corley, Elizabeth. *Tell Me about Death; Tell Me about Funerals.* Grammatical Sciences, 1973. (Ages 8–11)
  A gentle introduction to loss, funerals, and burial, this softcovered book is filled with down-to-earth information.

Grollman, Earl. *Talking about Death.* Boston: Beacon, 1971. (5+)
  Intended as part of a dialogue to take place between parent and child, the author warmly opens discussion in many sensitive areas.

Klagsbrun, Francine. *Too Young To Die: Youth and Suicide.* Boston: Houghton Mifflin, 1976. (12+)
  One of the leading causes of death among youth is examined.

Klein, Stanley, *The Final Mystery.* Garden City, New York: Doubleday, 1975. (8–13)
  Comparative religious practices, the life cycle, and humanity's fight against death are the focal points of this cross-cultural study.

Landau, Elaine. *Death: Everyone's Heritage.* New York: Messner, 1976. (12+)

Interviews with a dying person, someone who has attempted suicide, and someone who has lost a dear friend or relative are highlights of this book.

Langone, John. *Death Is a Noun.* Boston: Little, Brown, 1972. Dell, 1975. (12+)

Up-to-date research is the backbone of this readable examination of death's dilemmas: medical death, facing death, euthanasia, suicide, etc.

LeShan, Eda. *Learning to Say Good-by: When a Parent Dies.* New York: Macmillan, 1976. (8+)

The renowned psychologist discusses the death of a parent in depth.

——*What Makes Me Feel This Way?* New York: Macmillan, 1972. (8+)

One gentle chapter treats death and fear of dying most reassuringly.

Lifton, Robert Jay, and Olson, Eric. *Living and Dying.* New York: Praeger, 1974. (14+)

Fascinating, scholarly, and intellectually demanding, this historical overview investigates responses to death through the ages, concentrating most heavily upon the present nuclear age.

Lund, Doris. *Eric.* Philadelphia: Lippincott, 1974. (12+)

The story of a teenager's death from leukemia, movingly told by his mother.

Segerberg, Osborn, Jr. *Living with Death.* New York: Dutton, 1976. (12+)

Drawing from recent research, the author seeks to answer questions about death's mystery, the good death, and the good life that leads to it.

Simon, Seymour, *Life and Death in Nature.* New York: McGraw-Hill, 1976. (8–12)

The chain of life is investigated. In the decay of dead animal and plant life lies growth for a new generation.

Stein, Sarah. *About Dying.* New York: Walker, 1974. (4–9)

One narrative, for children, tells of plant, animal, and human death, as well as responses to death. The other, for parents, explains psychodynamics of loss reactions and urges honesty.

Turner, Ann. *Houses for the Dead: Burial Customs through the Ages*. New York: McKay, 1976. (12+)
 Burial rites, mourning beliefs and practices, funeral customs, ghost myths, and superstitions are discussed across time and many cultures.

Zim, Herbert, and Bleeker, Sonia. *Life and Death*. New York: Morrow, 1970. (8–12)
 The first nonfiction book about death for children, the Zims's book presents a calm, scientific explanation of the cycle of life and death. Customs around the world and comparative beliefs are also part of the book, which remains the classic in its field.

Books about Death: Fiction

Armstrong, William. *The Mills of God*. Garden City, New York: Doubleday, 1973. (Age 11+)
 A lonely boy, affected by the Depression and fatal illness of his brother, considers suicide when he must give up a beloved dog.

Arundel, Honor. *The Blanket Word*. Nashville: Nelson, 1973. (10–14)
 A girl's mother dies from cancer.

Asinof, Eliot. *Craig and Joan: Two Lives for Peace*. New York: Viking, 1971. (12–16)
 Two teens commit suicide in a peace pact.

Beckman, Gunnel. *Admission to the Feast*. New York: Holt, Rinehart and Winston, 1971. (12–16)
 A young woman reacts to the knowledge that she will die of leukemia.

Blue, Rose. *Nikki 108*. New York: Franklin Watts, 1973. (10–14)

A girl tries to overcome her environment, the setting in which her brother has died of an overdose.

Buck, Pearl. *The Big Wave.* New York: Day, 1948. (10+)
A look at terrible death instructs a youngster in the wonder of life. The eloquence and philosophy will enrich the reader.

Carrick, Carol. *The Accident.* New York: Seabury, 1976. (5–8)
After his dog is hit by a truck and killed, Christopher finds a satisfying way to express his grief and guilt.

Cleaver, Vera, and Cleaver, Bill. *Grover.* Philadelphia: Lippincott, 1970. (10–14)
The process of accepting a mother's suicide, chosen instead of a death from cancer.

Coburn, John. *Anne and the Sand Dobbies.* New York: Seabury, 1964. (8–12)
A religious account of death, as seen through the eyes of a young boy who loses his infant sister and dog.

Coutant, Helen. *First Snow.* New York: Knopf, 1974. (6–10)
Death as seen from the Buddhist point of view.

Dixon, Paige. *May I Cross Your Golden River?* New York: Atheneum, 1975. (12+)
Coping with a fatally ill sibling is the problem presented.

Donovan, John. *I'll Get There. It Better be Worth the Trip.* New York: Harper and Row, 1969. (12–16)
A lonely adolescent copes with changes in his life, including the death of his grandmother, with whom he lived, and relocation to live with his divorced, alcoholic mother.

———*Wild in the World.* New York: Harper and Row, 1971. (12–16)
In a household riddled by death, its last human survivor asks himself if fate determines survival.

Duncan, Lois. *I Know What You Did Last Summer.* Boston: Little, Brown, 1973. (12–16)
A suspenseful novel about a hidden hit-and-run accident.

Dunn, Mary. *The Man in the Box: A Story from Vietnam.* New York: McGraw-Hill, 1968. (12–16)
Friendship develops in the context of major loss.

Farley, Carol. *The Garden is Doing Fine.* New York: Atheneum, 1975. (12+)
A family garden symbolically represents attitudes toward dealing with tragedy.

Greene, Constance C. *Beat the Turtle Drum.* New York: Viking, 1976. (8–12)
This is the moving tale of the death of an eleven-year-old girl following an accident.

Guy, Rosa. *The Friends.* New York: Holt, Rinehart and Winston, 1973. (12–16)
The value of supportive friendship is investigaged through the character of a West Indian girl in a complex novel of urban life.

Hale, Janet. *The Owl's Song.* Garden City, New York: Doubleday, 1974. (12–16)
The problems of American Indian life unfold in the story of one young man's attempts to cope with poverty, alcoholism, and death.

Harden, Ruth. *High Pasture.* Boston: Houghton Mifflin, 1964. (9–14)
The difficulty of losing a mother to cancer is poignantly depicted.

Hautzig, Esther. *The Endless Steppe.* New York: Crowell, 1968. (12–16)
Hope and the realization that it is worse for others can keep a family going in wartime.

Heide, Florence. *Growing Anyway Up.* Philadelphia: Lippincott, 1965. (12–16)
Moving starts the process that brings understanding to a misfit teenager whose father has died.

Hinton, S. E. *The Outsiders.* New York: Viking, 1967. (12–16)

When families' bonds break down, close ties among peers can be helpful in fighting the battle for survival.

Holland, Isabelle. *Of Love and Death and Other Journeys.* Philadelphia: Lippincott, 1975. (12–16)
Cancer is a catalyst that brings about major alterations in Meg's lifestyle.

Kennedy, Richard. *Come Again in the Spring.* New York: Harper and Row, 1976. (6+)
Understanding of death derives from a parable about Old Hark and his adversary, Death.

Klein, Norma. *Confessions of an Only Child.* New York: Pantheon, 1974. (8–12)
The death of an infant and its effect upon a girl who did not want a sibling.

Lee, Mildred. *Fog.* New York: Seabury, 1972. (12–16)
Growing up after the death of one's father.

Lee, Virginia. *The Magic Moth.* New York: Seabury, 1972. (7–11)
A mystical account of a young girl's death.

L'Engle, Madeleine. *Meet the Austins.* New York: Vanguard, 1959. (10–13)
The loving harmony of the Austin household seems upset when the suddenly orphaned Maggy comes to live with them.

Little, Jean. *Home from Far.* Boston: Little, Brown, 1965. (8–12)
After a brother is killed in a car accident, Jenny's parents take in two foster children.

Mathis, Sharon Bell. *Listen for the Fig Tree.* New York: Viking, 1974. (12–16)
Muffin's pride in being black helps her cope with blindness, her father's murder, and her mother's alcoholic denial of that death.

Miles, Miska. *Annie and the Old One.* Boston: Little, Brown, 1971. (5–10)

Philosophical acceptance of old age and death on an Indian reservation.

Mohr, Nicholosa. *Nilda*. New York: Harper and Row, 1973. (12+)
Puerto Rican life in New York City during the 1940s is depicted through the eyes of an adolescent girl.

Moody, Ann. *Mister Death*. New York: Harper and Row, 1975. (12+)
Mississippi is the setting for four short stories in which death both terrifies and teaches about life.

Morgan, Alison. *Ruth Crane*. New York: Harper and Row, 1974. (12–16)
A vacation turns into a nightmare after a tragic auto crash.

Orgel, Doris. *The Mulberry Music*. New York: Harper and Row, 1971. (7–11)
Coping with the illness and death of a grandmother.

Platt, Kin. *Chloris and the Creeps*. Philadelphia: Chilton, 1973. (9–13)
The suicide of her father continues to cause severe problems for Chloris in this exploration of denial.

Rabin, Gil. *Changes*. New York: Harper and Row, 1973. (12–16)
This novel explores the impact of a sudden barrage of losses upon the life of an adolescent.

Rhodin, Eric. *The Good Greenwood*. Philadelphia: Westminster, 1971. (12–16)
An adolescent refuses to face the fact that his best friend has died.

Rockwell, Thomas. *Hiding Out*. Scarsdale, New York: Bradbury, 1974. (8–11)
Billy reacts turbulently to his mother's plan to remarry.

Simon, Shirley. *Libby's Step-Family*. New York: Lothrop, Lee and Shepard, 1966. (9–13)
Libby's mother remarries, and she suddenly loses her

closeness with her mother. Her gain doesn't seem positive: two uncooperative stepsisters.

Slote, Alfred. *Hang Tough, Paul Mather*. Philadelphia: Lippincott, 1973. (8–12)
   A boy faces the possibility of death from leukemia.

Smith, Doris. *A Taste of Blackberries*. New York: Crowell, 1973. (8–12)
   Coping with the death of a friend is difficult if you think you might have been able to prevent it.

Stevens, Carla. *Stories from a Snowy Meadow*. New York: Seabury, 1976. (6–9)
   When Old Vole dies, her young friends compose a song of tribute, expressing the joy they will take in their memory of her.

Stolz, Mary. *By the Highway Home*. New York: Harper and Row, 1971. (11–14)
   After the death of her brother in Vietnam, Catty's family becomes dejected and introspective.

Sypher, Lucy Johnston. *The Turnabout Year*. New York: Atheneum, 1976. (8–12)
   Lucy changes schools after being forced to come to terms with war and death.

Walker, Pamela. *Twyla*. Englewood Cliffs, New Jersey: Prentice-Hall, 1973. (11–16)
   Continually rejected, a mildly retarded misfit commits suicide.

Warburg, Sandol. *Growing Time*. Boston: Houghton-Mifflin, 1969. (6–9)
   Coping with the death of a dog and learning to understand life.

Wells, Rosemary. *None of the Above*. New York: Dial, 1974. (13+)
   Marcia's widowed father remarries; she is caught in a web of circumstances not to her liking.

Wersba, Barbara. *Run Softly, Go Fast.* New York: Atheneum, 1973. (12–16)
After his father dies, David reviews the love-hate relationship they shared.

Whitehead, Ruth. *The Mother Tree.* New York: Seabury, 1971. (8–12)
In helping a younger sister to grieve for their lost mother, Tempe facilitates her own mourning.

Wojciechowska, Maia. *Shadow of a Bull.* New York: Atheneum, 1964. (11–16)
Coping with legend is the theme of this novel.

———*Till the Break of Day.* New York: Harcourt, Brace, Jovanovich, 1972. (12–16)
The necessity for standing up to unjust invasion is a theme of this mature story of World War II.

Zindel, Paul. *The Pigman.* New York: Harper and Row, 1968. (12+)
Two teenagers taunt a grieving old man. Their treatment of him leads to their own bereavement.

Zolotow, Charlotte. *My Grandson Lew.* New York: Harper and Row, 1974. (4–8)
Lew is not told of his grandfather's death and waits for his return. He mourns him years later, as he and his mother evoke touching memories.

Advanced Study

Alsop, Stewart. *Stay of Execution.* Philadelphia: Lippincott, 1973.
American Friends Service Committee. *Who Shall Live? Man's Control Over Birth and Death.* New York: Hill and Wang, 1970.
Anthony, Sylvia. "The Child's Idea of Death." In *The World of the Child,* ed. by Toby Talbot. Garden City, New York: Doubleday, 1968 (Anchor edition).
———*The Discovery of Death in Childhood and After.* New York: Basic Books, 1972.
Arnstein, Helene. *What to Tell Your Child about Birth, Illness, Death, Divorce, and Family Crises.* Indianapolis: Bobbs-Merrill, 1962.
Association for Childhood Education International. *When Children Move from School to School.* Washington, D.C.: Author, 1972.
Bernstein, Joanne. *Helping Children Cope With Loss: A Bibliotherapy Approach.* New York: Bowker, 1977.
Caine, Lynn. *Widow.* New York: Morrow, 1974.
Callahan, Sidney. *The Working Mother.* New York: Macmillan, 1971.
Carr, Austin C., and others. *Grief: Selected Readings.* New York: Health Sciences, 1973.
Cook, Sarah, ed. *Children and Dying.* New York: Health Sciences, 1973.
Cutter, Fred. *Coming to Terms with Death.* New York: Nelson-Hall, 1974.
Debuskey, Matthew, and Dombro, Robert, eds. *The Chron-*

ically Ill Child and His Family. Springfield, Illinois: Charles C. Thomas, 1970.

Dempsey, David. *The Way We Die*. New York: Macmillan, 1975.

Draznin, Yaffa. *How to Prepare for Death*. New York: Hawthorn, 1976.

Easson, William. *The Dying Child: The Management of the Child or Adolescent Who Is Dying*. Springfield, Illinois: Charles C. Thomas, 1970.

Farberow, N. L. *Suicide and Suicide Prevention. Bibliography*. Washington, D.C.: U.S. Printing Office, 1971.

Feifel, Herman, ed. *The Meaning of Death*. New York: McGraw-Hill, 1959.

Flandorf, V. S. *Books to Help Children Adjust to a Hospital Situation*. Chicago: American Library Association, 1967.

Geddes, Joan Bel. *How to Parent Alone: A Guide for Single Parents*. New York: Seabury, 1974.

Geist, Harold. *A Child Goes to the Hospital: The Psychological Aspects of a Child Going to the Hospital*. Springfield, Illinois: Charles C. Thomas, 1965.

Gorer, Geoffrey. *Death: Grief and Mourning*. Garden City, New York: Doubleday, 1956.

Grollman, Earl, ed. *Explaining Death to Children*. Boston: Beacon Press, 1967.

———*Concerning Death: A Practical Guide for the Living*. Boston: Beacon Press, 1976.

Hendin, David. *Death as a Fact of Life*. New York: Warner, 1974.

Hinton, John. *Dying*. Baltimore: Penguin Books, 1967.

Jackson, Edgar N. *Telling a Child about Death*. New York: Channel Press, 1965.

Kastenbaum, Robert, and Aisenberg, Ruth. *The Psychology of Death*. New York: Springer Publishing, 1972.

Kavanaugh, Robert. *Facing Death*. Baltimore: Penguin, 1973.

Keleman, Stanley. *Living Your Dying*. New York: Random House, 1975.

Kelley, Marjorie E. *In Pursuit of Values: A Bibliography of*

Children's Books. Ramsey, New Jersey: Paulist Press, 1973.

Klein, Carole. *The Single Parent Experience*. New York: Walker Publishing, 1973.

Kliman, Gilbert. *Psychological Emergencies of Childhood*. New York: Grune and Stratton, 1968.

Krant, Melvin J. *Dying and Dignity: The Meaning and Control of a Personal Death*. Springfield, Illinois: Charles C. Thomas, 1974.

Kübler-Ross, Elisabeth. *On Death and Dying*. New York: Macmillan, 1969.

———*Questions and Answers on Death and Dying*. New York: Macmillan, 1974.

Kübler-Ross, Elisabeth, ed. *Death: The Final Stage of Growth*. Englewood Cliffs, New Jersey: Prentice-Hall, 1975.

Kutscher, Austin H., ed. *Death and Bereavement*. Springfield, Illinois: Charles C. Thomas, 1969.

———*But Not to Lose: A Book of Comfort for Those Bereaved*. New York: Frederick Fell, 1969.

Kutscher, Austin, and Goldberg, M. *Caring for the Dying Patient and His Family*. New York: Health Sciences, 1973.

Langone, John. *Vital Signs: The Way We Die in America*. Boston: Little, Brown, 1974.

LeShan, Eda. *The Wonderful Crisis of Middle Age: Some Personal Reflections*. New York: McKay, 1973.

Lewis, Alfred, with Barrie Berns. *Three Out of Four Wives: Widowhood in America*. New York: Macmillan, 1975.

Lifton, Robert Jay. *Death in Life: Survivors of Hiroshima*. New York: Random House, 1967.

Love, Harold D., Henderson, Shirley, and Stewart, Mary. *Your Child Goes to the Hospital: A Book for Parents*. Springfield, Illinois: Charles C. Thomas, 1972.

Maddox, Brenda. *The Half-Parent*. New York: Evans, 1975.

Maguire, Daniel. *Death by Choice*. Garden City, New York: Doubleday, 1974.

Marris, Peter. *Loss and Change*. New York: Pantheon Books, 1974.

Mitchell, Marjorie. *The Child's Attitude to Death.* New York: Schocken, 1967.
Moody, Mildred T., and Limper, Hilda K. *Bibliotherapy: Methods and Materials.* Chicago: American Library Association, 1971.
Moody, Raymond A., Jr. *Life After Life.* Covington, Georgia: Mockingbird, 1976.
Moriarty, David, ed. *The Loss of Loved Ones: The Effects of a Death in the Family on Personality Development.* Springfield, Illinois: Charles C. Thomas, 1967.
Neale, Robert. *The Art of Dying.* New York: Harper and Row, 1973.
Ogden, Gina, and Zevin, Anne. *When a Family Needs Therapy.* Boston: Beacon, 1976.
Phipps, Joyce. *Death's Single Privacy: Grieving and Personal Growth.* New York: Seabury, 1974.
Pincus, Lily. *Death and the Family: The Importance of Mourning.* New York: Pantheon, 1975.
Riggs, Corinne, comp., Raymond Ross, gen. ed. *Bibliotherapy: An Annotated Bibliography.* Newark, Delaware: International Reading Association, 1971.
Ruina, Edith. *Moving: A Common-Sense Guide to Relocating Your Family.* New York: Funk and Wagnalls, 1970.
Russell, O. Ruth. *Freedom to Die.* New York: Dell, 1976.
Schneidman, Edwin. *Deaths of Man.* New York: Quadrangle Press, 1973.
Schneidman, Edwin S., ed. *Suicidology: Contemporary Developments.* New York: Grune and Stratton, 1976.
Schulman, Jerome. *Coping with Tragedy: Successfully Facing the Problem of a Seriously Ill Child.* Chicago: Follett, 1976.
Schultheis, Sister Miriam. *A Guidebook for Bibliotherapy.* Glenview, Illinois: Psychotechnics, 1972.
Silverman, Phyllis, and others. *Helping Each Other in Widowhood.* New York: Health Sciences, 1974.
Simon, Anne. *Stepchild in the Family: A View of Children in Remarriage.* Indianapolis: Odyssey Press, 1964.

Start, Clarissa. *When You're a Widow.* St. Louis: Concordia Publishing House, 1968.

Stengel, E. *Suicide and Attempted Suicide.* Baltimore: Pelican, 1967.

Strugnell, Cecile. *Adjustment to Widowhood and Some Related Problems.* New York: Health Sciences, 1973.

Tanner, Ira. *The Gift of Grief: Healing the Pain of Everyday Losses.* New York: Hawthorn, 1976.

Thomson, Helen. *The Successful Stepparent.* New York: Harper and Row, 1966.

Weisman, Avery. *On Dying and Denying.* New York: Behavioral Publications, 1972.

Williams, Robert H., ed. *To Live and to Die: When, Why, and How.* New York: Springer-Verlag, 1973.

Wolf, Anna M. *Helping Your Child to Understand Death,* rev. ed. New York: Child Study Press, 1973.

Wolfenstein, Martha, and Kliman, Gilbert, eds. *Children and the Death of a President.* Garden City, New York: Doubleday, 1965.

Wolff, Sula. *Children Under Stress.* Baltimore: Penguin, 1969.

Worden, J. William. *P.D.A.: Personal Death Awareness.* Englewood Cliffs, New Jersey: Prentice-Hall, 1976.

Zaccaria, Joseph, and Moses, Harold. *Facilitating Human Development Through Reading: The Use of Bibliotherapy in Teaching and Counseling.* Champaign, Illinois: Stipes, 1968.

Zeligs, Rose. *Children's Experience with Death.* Springfield, Illinois: Charles C. Thomas, 1974.

Films about Death

"Death, the Enemy."
  Psychology Today Reader Service,
  Box 700, Dept. ID, Del Mar, California, 92014
    Seminar on death and dying. Cassette and reading anthology. Robert Jay Lifton, Edwin Schneidman, and others contribute ideas about death in contemporary society.

"How Could I Not Be Among You: The Poetry of Ted Rosenthal."
  Eccentric Circle Cinema Workshop,
  P.O. Box 1481, Evanston, Ill., 60204
    A young artist expresses his response to terminal illness.

"Living with Dying."
  Sunburst Communications,
  Hemlock Hill Road, Pound Ridge, New York, 10576
    Two 15-minute sound filmstrips, each with phonodiscs or cassettes plus guide, introduce the subject with honesty.

"Perspectives on Death."
  Educational Perspectives Associates,
  P.O. Box 213, De Kalb, Illinois, 60115
    Anthology of reading for secondary school students. Student activity book, teacher's resource book, plus filmstrips and tape cassettes are included. Death is explored cross-culturally and in historical perspective.

"Room and Board."
  Malibu Films,
  Box 428, Malibu, California, 90265

A provocative (5-minute) metaphoric film that deals with life and death; secondary school students and adults will offer many interpretations of the protagonist's attempts to open a single door.

"Though I Walk Through the Valley."
  Pyramid Films,
  Box 1048, Santa Monica, California, 90406
    Tony Brouwer, a man facing death, finds support in religious belief. The 30-minute documentary of his life and feelings will touch and inform.

"Understanding Death."
  Educational Perspectives Associates,
  Box 213, De Kalb, Illinois, 60115
    This series for upper elementary grades includes four filmstrips with cassette narrations, a teacher's guide, plus a filmstrip and cassette that instructs parents and teachers about death education.

"Chickamauga"
  Contemporary Films/McGraw-Hill, Inc.
  Princeton Road
  Hightstown, New Jersey, 08520
    After surviving deafness and the ravages of war, a young boy begins to comprehend the reality of death as it relates to him personally. Filmed in black and white.

"Death"
  Extension Media Center
  University of California
  Berkeley, California, 94720
    In little more than half an hour, a poignant journey into the dying experience of one cancer patient convinces viewers of the necessity to embrace life.

"The Day Grandpa Died"
  King Screen Productions
  320 Aurora Avenue North
  Seattle, Washington, 98109
    This twelve-minute color short stresses being able to look

at loss from varying viewpoints. The ten-year-old protagonist is told, "You lost a grandfather; I lost a father."

"Children in Crisis"
Parents' Magazine Films, Inc.
52 Vanderbilt Avenue
New York, New York, 10017

Four sound and color filmstrips comprise this series. They focus upon child abuse and neglect, death, illness, and divorce. Aimed at parents and professionals, the set is available with records or cassettes.

"You See . . . I've Already Had a Life"
Temple University
Philadelphia, Pennsylvania

A thirteen-year-old leukemic boy discusses his feelings about illness, depression, isolation, and death.

"Omega"
Pyramid Films
Box 1048
Santa Monica, California, 90406

Laden with special effects, Omega attempts to be the last word in color shorts. For thirteen minutes, those who watch will be transported into the imagined imagery of existence after death.

Service Organizations and Sources for Information

American Association of Psychiatric Clinics for Children, 250 West 57th Street, New York, New York, 10019
   This is a good source for information about referrals.

American Association of Suicidology, Suicide Prevention Center, 220 West 26th Avenue, San Mateo, California, 94403
   Dedicated to research and the prevention of unnecessary deaths, this organization offers membership, information, and counseling information.

American Cancer Society,
777 Third Avenue, New York, New York, 10019
   Rehabilitation, counseling for families, and research are the interests of the Society.

American Heart Association,
44 East 23rd Street, New York, New York, 10010
   Consultation and published information are available concerning the leading killer of adults in the United States.

American Orthopsychiatric Association,
1790 Broadway, New York, New York, 10019
   Interested in a wide range of problems, this organization is a good source for technical information about children in contemporary society.

Association for Childhood Education International,
3615 Wisconsin Avenue, N.W., Washington, D.C., 20016
> Interested in the education and upbringing of children under age twelve, the Association publishes many books, booklets, and manuals about emotional and psychological well-being.

Cancer Care, Inc.,
1 Park Avenue, New York, New York, 10016
> Counseling of families and education of the public are available.

The Candlelighters,
123 C Street, S.E., Washington, D.C., 20003
> A national organization of groups of parents of children who have had or do have cancer. They help one another, keep informed of research programs, and lobby to conquer cancer.

Center for Death Education and Research,
University of Minnesota, Minneapolis, Minnesota, 55455
> Many scholarly and nontechnical publications are available from this organization, as well as film strips and cassettes.

Child Study Association,
50 Madison Avenue, New York, New York, 10010
> Geared toward healthful child-raising and family life, the Child Study Association publishes manuals, booklets, and bibliographies of helpful reading for both adults and young people.

Child Welfare League,
67 Irving Place, New York, New York, 10003
> Particularly interested in children in distress, this organization publishes many materials for professionals and interested parents.

Continental Association of Funeral and Memorial Societies,
50 East Van Buren Street, Chicago, Illinois.

Information concerning the cost and conduct of funerals is available.

Equinox Institute,
11 Clinton Street, Brookline, Massachusetts, 02146
Dr. Melvin Krant, the director of the Institute is a leading researcher in thanatology. His Institute helps both the dying and their survivors learn to cope.

Euthanasia Educational Council,
250 West 57th Street, New York, New York, 10019
Promoting the right to die with dignity, the Council distributes information, runs study courses, and helps individuals toward open discussion of death.

Family Service Association of America,
44 East 23rd Street, New York, New York, 10010
This organization is geared toward helping families under stress.

Alan Foss Leukemia Memorial Fund,
730 East 79th Street, Brooklyn, New York, 11236
This person-to-person care program helps families with terminally ill members. Supporting research, providing economic aid to families, and giving emotional aid are three of its goals.

Foundation of Thanatology,
630 West 168th Street, New York, New York, 10032
Conferences and publications about bereavement are aimed at both general audiences and professionals concerned with loss.

Highly Specialized Promotions,
20 Schermerhorn Street, Brooklyn, New York, 11201
Roberta Halporn's book promotion service deals exclusively with published materials about loss and grief. She offers a thanatology bibliography, as well as exhibits at conferences.

Horizons in the Life Cycle, Inc.,
490 Riverside Drive, New York, New York, 10027

As the last segment of the life cycle, death is a focus of this organization, which provides educational materials and counseling referrals.

Hospice, Inc.,
765 Prospect Street, New Haven, Connecticut, 06511
The British originated the concept of a hospital where one goes to die peacefully. The movement is spreading to this country.

Information Center on the Mature Woman,
515 Madison Avenue, New York, New York, 10022
Covering health, economics, sociology, psychology, and leisure, this Center publicizes news and research concerning mature women. It also provides a speakers' service and radio programs.

International Guild for Infant Survival,
6822 Brompton Road, Baltimore, Maryland, 21207
This organization works toward elimination of Sudden Infant Death Syndrome and education of the public.

Life Extension Society
2011 N. St., N.W., Washington, D.C., 20036
Some people believe that if we are frozen immediately following death, we can be unfrozen and live at a later date. This group fosters the practice, called cryogenic storage.

Living Bank
1017 Hawthorne, P.O. Box 6725, Houston, Texas, 77005
Coordinating the disposition of gifts of body organs, this nonprofit clearinghouse registers prospective donors.

Mental Health Materials Center,
419 Park Avenue South, New York, New York, 10016
The Center will provide reading matter and information concerning health professionals.

National Association for Mental Health,
1800 N. Kent Street, Rosslyn, Virginia, 22209
The Association publishes material concerning grief and provides advice about referrals.

National Council of Family Relations,
1219 University Avenue, S.E., Minneapolis, Minnesota, 55415
> Families under stress can find information and referrals here.

National Foundation for Sudden Infant Death, Inc.
1501 Broadway, New York, New York, 10036
> Concentrating upon research and dissemination of findings, this group also runs family discussion groups and local chapters.

National Funeral Directors Association,
135 West Wells Street, Milwaukee, Wisconsin, 53202
> Educational materials concerning funeral planning and problems of bereavement are available.

National Society for Medical Research,
111 Fourth Street, S.E., Rochester, Minnesota
> Information concerning procedures for donating body organs is available.

Parents Without Partners,
7910 Woodmont Avenue, Washington, D.C., 20014
> Single parents and their children find activities and comfort through this national organization. Discussion groups for adolescents are formed.

Public Affairs Pamphlets,
381 Park Avenue South, New York, New York, 10016
> Many inexpensive publications offer suggestions for dealing with crisis. Among those recommended: #269—"When you Lose a Loved One," #287—"The One Parent Family," #406A—"Dealing with the Crisis of Suicide," #485—"The Dying Person and the Family" (35¢ each).

Society of Compassionate Friends,
27 A Street, Columbus Close, Coventry CV1, 4 BX, Warwickshire, England
> The parents of leukemic and other terminally ill children seek help here.

Widow-to-Widow Program,
Laboratory of Community Psychiatry, 58 Fernwood Road, Boston, Massachusetts, 02115

> In this pioneering program, widows help one another adjust to the impact of loss.

Life Events Scale

Life Change	Scale of Impact
1. Death of Spouse	100
2. Divorce	73
3. Marital separation	65
4. Jail term	63
5. Death of close family member	63
6. Personal injury or illness	53
7. Marriage	50
8. Fired at work	47
9. Marital reconciliation	45
10. Retirement	45
11. Change in health of family member	44
12. Pregnancy	40
13. Sex difficulties	39
14. New family member	39
15. Business readjustment	39
16. Change in financial status	38
17. Death of close friend	37
18. Change to different line of work	36
19. Change in number of arguments with spouse	35
20. Mortgage over $10,000	31
21. Foreclosure of mortgage or loan	30
22. Change in responsibilities at work	29
23. Son or daughter leaving home	29
24. Trouble with in-laws	29
25. Outstanding personal achievement	28

Life Change	Scale of Impact
26. Wife begins or stops work	26
27. Begin or end school	26
28. Change in living conditions	25
29. Revision of personal habits	24
30. Trouble with boss	23
31. Change in work hours or conditions	20
32. Change in residence	20
33. Change in schools	20
34. Change in recreation	19
35. Change in church activities	19
36. Change in social activities	18
37. Mortgage or loan less than $10,000	17
38. Change in sleeping habits	16
39. Change in number of family reunions	15
40. Change in eating habits	15
41. Vacation	13
42. Christmas	12
43. Minor violations of the law	11

Index

Absent mourning, 42-43
Acceptance
  of death, 45-64, 98
  in terminal illness, 88, 89
Accidental deaths, 82-83
Alaskan Indians, 90
Anger, 8, 35-39, 72
  expression of, 50-51
  of survivors, 73, 97
  in terminal illness, 88
  turned inward, 37-39
Animals, reincarnation as, 16
Anticipatory grief, 85-86
Asinof, Eliot, 92
Aunt, death of, 69-70

Bacon, Francis, 59
Bargaining in terminal illness, 86, 88
Bereavement (grief), 31-35
  anticipatory, 85-86
  decision making minimized during, 107-8
  depression in, 41-42
  family quarrels about, 97
  healing of, 55-60, 65
  as opportunity, 120
  pain of, 32, 33, 40, 47-48, 54-55, 106-7
  Shakespeare on, 82
  successful, 45-64
  therapy in, 60-64
  See also Mourning
Bible, the, 56
Ecclesiastes, 9, 17
Books, *see* Reading
Bradbury, Ray, 53-54, 111
Brain, death of, 4-5
Breakdown, life events scale and, 105
Brother, death of, 78-81
Burial, 10-11

Cadavers for medical schools, 110-11
Casket, 8, 10
"Catching death," 95
Catholics, 15
Cavett, Dick, 71-72
Cemetery, 10-11, 12
Checkup needed by survivors, 105-6
Christianity, 15
Circle of life, 15

Index

Clergy, 60
Cluster families, 102-4
Columbarium, 11
Condolence call, 16-17
Counselor, 60
Coutant, Helen, *First Snow,* 12
Craig and Joan: Two Lives for Peace (Asinof), 92
Cremation, 11-12
Crib death, 84-85

Dark Carnival (Bradbury), 53
Death
  children's envisioning of, 41, 53
  children's ideas about, 18-24, 39
  definition of, 4-5
  denial of, 25-26, 34-35, 49
  as embarrassment, 26-28, 38, 71-72
  fear of, 8, 13, 39-41, 79
  as frustrating, 50-52
  harmony in, 13
  misinformation about, 28-30
  need to talk about, 56-57, 59
  See also specific topics
Death-angel (death-man), 23, 24
Death certificates, 7
Defiance of death in terminal illness, 90
Delayed mourning, 42-43
Denial
  of death, 25-26, 34-35, 49
  in terminal illness, 87, 89
Depression, 41-42
  before suicide, 93
  in terminal illness, 88
Donne, John, 17
Dreams, dead people in, 34

Eastern religions, 15-16
Ecclesiastes, 9, 17
Embalming, 7, 11
Embarrassment about death, 26-28, 38, 71-72
Expecting too much of survivors, 101-2

Facilitation of death in terminal illness, 89-90
Families
  cluster, 102-4
  after a death, 96-102, 108
  reconciliation of, 118
Farm, life and death cycle of, 26
Fantasy deaths, 41, 53
Fear of death, 8, 13, 39-41, 79
Films about death, 135-37
Financial problems after a death, 104
Firefighters, anticipatory mourning for, 85
First Snow (Coutant), 12
Friend, death of, 68-69
Funeral, 5-10
  family fight over, 97
  pet's, 67

Funeral directors, 6-7
Funeral home, 7

Games
　"death," 66-67
　separation, 19
God
　anger at, 37
　bargaining with, 86
　death and, 15, 29-30
Grandparent, death of, 69-70
Grief, *see* Bereavement
Grollman, Earl, 47
Guardians, parents' provision for, 52-53
Guilt, 37-38, 52, 54, 80, 98
　over accidental deaths, 83
　after suicide, 94
Gullo, Dr. Stephen, 89

Halo creation around dead person, 98-99
Hansel and Gretel, 77
Heart disease from mourning, 104
Heaven, 14-15
Heritage, 111-13, 119
Hiding as reaction to death, 23
Hindus, 15-16
Holmes, Dr. Thomas, 105
Horror stories, purpose of, 53-54
Hospital, death in, 26-27

Identity, examination of one's, 119

Illness
　in bereavement, 33, 40, 47-48
　from strain of mourning, 104-8
　suicide because of, 93
　terminal, 38-39, 68, 79, 80-81, 85-91
Immortality, 14-16
Infants, crib death of, 84-85
Information, sources for, list of, 138-43
Inheritances, 109-10, 115-16

Jews, 15

Kavanaugh, Robert, 87
Kennedy, John, 23
Killings, 83
　in the media, 28
Koocher, Gerald, 23
Kota Indian tribe, 6
Krant, Dr. Melvin, 104
Kübler-Ross, Dr. Elisabeth, 13, 87-90

Lee, Virginia, *The Magic Moth,* 14, 79
Legacies, 109-10, 115-16
L'Engle, Madeleine, 34
Leukemia, 23, 38
Life events scale, 105, 144-45
Life cycle, 15-16, 26, 30
Love, fear of, 50

Magic Moth, The (Lee), 14, 79
Marcus Aurelius, 4

Index

Marie de France, 119
"M*A*S*H," 50-51
Mausoleum, 11
Medical schools, cadavers for, 110-11
Memorial meeting, 5-6, 8
Memories of dead persons, 113-15
Methodists, 30
Mills, John, 120
Misinformation about death, 28-30
Moody, Dr. Raymond, 13
Morticians, 6-7
Mourning
  absent or delayed, 42-43
  anticipatory, 85-86
  a definition of, 47
  energy needed for, 106
  hindered by too many interests, 106
  lessons from, 117-20
  on-again-off-again, 43-44
  strain of, 104-8
  by surviving parent, 71
  See also Bereavement
Movies, 27-28
  about death, 135-37
Murder, 83
My Grandson Lew (Zolotow), 56

Nagy, Maria, 20, 23, 24
Near dead people who have lived, 13, 14
"Nearness" of dead person, 35

Overprotection of survivors, 81, 99-101

Pain of bereavement, 32, 33, 40, 47-48, 54-55, 106-7
Parent
  death of, 70-75
  provision for child by, 52-53
  remarriage of, 75-78
  and surviving child, 81, 99-102
Parents Without Partners, 103
Parkes, Dr. Murray, 104
Peek-a-boo, 19
Pets, death of, 66-67
Plato, 14
Police officers, anticipatory mourning for, 85
Property of dead person, 110
Protestants, 15
Psychiatrists, 60, 62
Psychologists, 60, 62
Punishment, survivor's seeking of, 52

Reading
  for healing, 58-60
  further, 121, 34
Reality testing, 47-49
Reconciliation, 118
Rejection, death as, 39
Relief at death of a person, 39
Religious beliefs, 15-16, 29-30
Remarriage of parent, 75-78
Remorse, 37

"Rest in peace," 25
Russell, Bertrand, 50

Samoa, 11
Schowalter, John, 10, 70-71
Sedatives, 107
Self-destructive behavior, 93
Separations, 18-20
Service organizations, list of, 138-43
Sexual contact between parent and surviving child, 101-2
Shakespeare, William, 82
Sharing beds with parents, 101-2
Sharing of memories, 56-57
Shock in terminal illness, 87
Shock of survivors, 6
   at accidental or violent deaths, 82-83
Short sadness span, 44
Sibling, death of, 78-81
SIDS (Sudden Infant Death Syndrome), 84-85
Single-parent families, 72-75
Sister, death of, 78-81
Smith, Doris Buchanan, *A Taste of Blackberries*, 112
Smoking during mourning, 107
Snow White, 77
Snowflakes, 12
Social worker, 60
Soul, 12-13
Stepparents, 75-78
Submission in terminal illness, 89
Suicide, 91-95

Talking about one's bereavement, 56-57, 59
Talmud, 113
Taste of Blackberries, A (Smith), 112
Television, 27-28, 50, 65
Terminal illness, 38-39, 68, 79, 80-81, 85-91
Thanatologists, 32, 87
Therapy, 60-64
Time for healing, 55-60, 65
Toilets, children's interest in, 20
Traditions, 111-13
Tranquilizers, 107
Transcendence of death in terminal illness, 90
Trash cans, children's interest in, 20

Uncle, death of, 69-70
Undertakers, 6-7
Urn garden, 11

Vietnam War, protest suicides during, 92
Violent deaths, 82-83

Walker, Pamela, *Twyla*, 60
War, death in, 85
Wedding, denial of death at, 49
Weeping, Bible on, 56

Wills, 109-10, 52-53
Wolfenstein, Dr. Martha, 44

Zolotow, Charlotte, *My Grandson Lew*, 56